RENT TO
KILL

DREW DUNMOORE

RENT TO KILL

This book is dedicated to my sweet friend Grace. May you rest in peace. I'm so sorry you didn't get to read this. I think you would have loved it. Thanks for laughing at all my jokes and always reading my notes in school. You are loved my friend, and I'll meet you on the other side someday…past the lockers…past the lunch lines…and right into eternity.

Jennifer

It was already 85°F at 9:30 in the morning. It would be another hot August day in Sunshine Beach, California. Jennifer Riley, a hot one too, set out that morning to tan herself on the rooftop observation deck of the building she resided in. Regal Palms, erected in 1958, was a gem that stood twelve stories tall in the middle of the city.

Jennifer stretched out on a wicker lawn chair and misted herself with a spray bottle, the kind with a little fan connected to the spout. She blew air onto her pretty face and sprayed her beautiful body. As she felt cool little droplets of tap water land on her slender limbs, she admired how they glistened in the sunlight on her perfectly bronzed skin. Jennifer loved her long legs. At times she used them as bait, or a weapon, depending on her mood.

Sun rays glittered on the swaying palm trees rooted in the ground on the street below, and there wasn't a cloud in the sky. The roof heated up to a nice sizzling temperature while Jennifer heard the traffic hum along on the road below. A slight smell of smog and salt air seeped into her nostrils. She slinked into her tiniest bikini that morning—a little green stringy thing that barely covered her implants. She staked out a prime spot on the observation deck, because others in the building would be up there soon.

Having lived in the building for several years, Jennifer acquired an array of single men that had their eye on her…and some married ones too. Jennifer delighted herself in them all. She loved the attention, the gifts, and the affection. In the summertime, lots of men in the building sauntered up to the roof to check her out—an observation deck indeed!

That morning she sat alone and waited to be seen. She loved to be seen. With her scantily clad rear end stuck to the lawn chair, she pulled her blond hair into a ponytail. She closed her eyes. Her skin roasted to perfection in the California summer sun. For a moment, as she sat there twelve stories above the world, and twelve stories closer to heaven, she thought the sun moved behind a cloud, because it got just a little cooler. Then, she remembered there were no clouds out. She pulled off her sunglasses and saw who blocked her sun. She asked, "What do you want now?" Her admirer heard the snotty tone in her voice. She waited for a response, and a snarl crept over her face that made her new nose job look a little less than perfect.

Those were the last words Jennifer Riley spoke, because the shadow moved closer and got colder. Before she could get away, a strong hand firmly gripped her throat. Her windpipe closed. She tried to breathe but couldn't. Blood vessels in her face began to burst. Her eyes watered. Her mind panicked. Her legs kicked involuntarily. She tasted salty tears right before everything went black.

Seconds later, Jennifer Riley's bones met the asphalt on the street twelve stories below. The hand of fate pushed her down, twelve stories closer to hell.

Chapter One

The Phone Tree

The cream of wheat bubbled in the old red and white enamel pot as Maybel Morgan stirred it lovingly, just like she did every Saturday morning for the last fifty-nine years. Dean Martin sang from the record player, as she added butter and cinnamon to the pot. The only thing missing from her ritual was her husband George. After he passed away, Maybel felt in her heart his breakfast tradition must continue, as her effort to keep his memory alive. She set a place for George at her yellow Formica table. The windows next to her table gifted her with a spectacular view of the north side of Sunshine Beach, where she lived since 1958. Even though so much time passed, for Maybel Morgan, not much changed inside the condo she lived in.

She served George's favorite breakfast to herself. The daisies in the middle of the table brought a smile to her face, as she remembered how once a week George brought them home to her. She never had the heart to tell him daisies weren't her favorite flower, but now that he passed, they were her favorite flower. She buttered a piece of toast and thought about how much she missed him. She even missed picking up his dirty socks. "George, I'm not your mother," she would remind him, but the truth was, she loved taking care of him.

After all the dishes from breakfast were cleaned up, she planned to sit in her den and work on her knitting. Those plans were thwarted by a phone call from a tenant in the building. The leaves of the Regal Palms phone tree rustled, and her touch tone phone in her kitchen rang. Her and George upgraded to it from a rotary phone back in the 80's…what a luxury she often thought. She shut off the faucet and wiped her hands on the blue embroidered apron tied around her hourglass waist.

Maybel clutched her chest and said into the phone, "Oh, good heavens! I'll be right down!"

Maybel clutched her chest and said into the phone, "Oh, good heavens! I'll be right down!"

As she hurried out of her condo on the ninth floor, she passed a picture hanging in the hallway. The image of the good shepherd watching over his flock was a favorite of hers. She didn't think to lock her door, because she trusted her neighbors. Maybel punched the down arrow button on the elevator and waited…and waited. "Oh, this stupid thing!" She kicked the door with her orthopedic shoe. A minute later, the doors opened, and she hurried in and hit the lobby button. The elevator's descent stopped abruptly on the fifth floor with a clunk. "Damn it," she mumbled under her breath as the doors opened.

Vick Arnold, President of the Regal Palms Homeowners Association, greeted her with a slight nod of his head that almost touched the top of the elevator door. "Maybel," he said tersely.

Maybel pursed her lips. "Vick," she said curtly. "You don't need to hit that button! I already did," Maybel continued, "Nice to see they contacted you after they contacted me."

"What makes you think they contacted you first?" Vick asked.

"What makes you think they didn't? Everyone knows who is really in charge around here." Maybel and her husband George were one of the original co-op owners, before Regal Palms converted to condominiums. For many years, she felt it her duty to serve on the board for the people of Regal Palms, and she believed herself to be the best board president Regal Palms tenants ever had. As the self-proclaimed matriarch of the building, she served the people faithfully for years.

Vick disagreed and said, "This building is thriving under my leadership, Maybel. There is no more frivolous spending, because I run a tight ship. Everyone knows I'm the best president."

Maybel snorted and said, "Well, then you're the worst at what you think you do the best!" She turned and fluffed her curly silver hair in the elevator mirror.

"Do I need to remind you that you were asked to step down as board President?" Vick asked eluding to a prior, slight political scandal involving Maybel and Vick's father.

With ruffled feathers, Maybel shouted, "Do I need to remind you that nobody likes you!?" She jumped out of the elevator ahead of him. "Try to keep up!" She called out over her should as she scurried through the lobby, which also hadn't changed much since 1958. She barreled out the double glass doors with Vick right behind her. Several neighbors were already out on the street. She gathered information from them, while Vick approached the barricade the police set up around Jennifer Riley's body. Not to be outdone, Maybel quickly made her way to the barricade.

From what Maybel could see, the head detective seemed to be very forthcoming with Vick. Probably because he's a man, Maybel thought. She aggressively pushed her way through the crowd. Her age never slowed her down. She asked the detective if there was anything she could do to help.

Vick said in a commanding tone, "Maybel! We've got this. Why don't you go back upstairs and watch your programs on TV?"

Maybel huffed off but not before getting a good look at Jennifer's body. They covered it up, but she could see one of Jennifer's legs sticking out. Maybel felt a bit sick to her stomach seeing this and decided it was a good idea to go back inside. She wanted to let her neighbor Celeste know what transpired.

Celeste Ravenna lived on the ninth floor next to Maybel Morgan, and Maybel thought of Celeste as the daughter she never had. Celeste, having lost her mother at a young age, embraced Maybel's motherly tendencies towards her. The hurt Celeste felt over her loss never left her. In their hearts, Celeste and Maybel's friendship worked quite well.

As she heard the knock, Celeste sipped coffee in her kitchen and was already showered and ready for the day. Celeste had the dark eyes of gypsy that could see all your secrets. "Maybel, what are you doing here so early? It's not time for lunch yet," Celeste said referring to the standing lunch date her and Maybel kept every Saturday—a tradition that started when Celeste befriended Maybel after George passed.

Maybel spoke quickly, "Something horrible happened this morning. Jennifer committed suicide and jumped off the roof! Landed in the middle of the street smack dab on Pacific Boulevard!"

"Jennifer?" Celeste asked.

Maybel looked slightly annoyed Celeste could never remember anyone in the building. Maybel, however, prided herself on knowing everyone and finding out as much as she possibly could about each person. "You know," Maybel paused, "that trollop that lived on the third floor. I mean, God rest her soul, but she was a tramp." Maybel whispered, "She'd slept with the entire fifth floor."

Celeste gave a confused look to Maybel and asked, "But I thought you said she lived on the third floor?"

Maybel mused, "She must have been trying to work her way up." She continued, "Do you really not remember her? She was the buxom blond who stood up at the last HOA meeting and said she had no hot water in her shower. Vick took one look at her, and he started breathing heavy. Then, he looked like *he* needed the cold shower…if you know what I mean."

Celeste sipped more coffee and asked, "How do you know she slept with the entire fifth floor?" Celeste was not part of the phone tree that sometimes threw shade on the tenants of Regal Palms.

"Don't worry about it," Maybel waived her off and continued, "I wonder why that poor girl would jump off the roof. The police are out there right now cleaning up." Maybel went on, "Everything is taped off. There's a huge crowd of people standing around, and traffic is all backed up. What a horrific scene…"

Celeste asked, "How did you get close enough to see if there is a crowd out there and everything is taped off?"

Maybel replied, "Don't worry about it, darling. That doesn't matter now. Both of her legs were broken and bent up—just a twisted awful sight!" She lowered her voice again and continued, "Someone even said her implants ruptured on impact."

"Oh, geez…that's horrible! It might not even be true. Maybe you shouldn't repeat that," Celeste warned.

"Well, I've only said it to you, and you never talk to anyone in the building except for me," Maybel said.

Celeste tried to remember Jennifer. A vague recollection of Jennifer popped into her mind. She'd seen her in the lobby a few times and at the HOA meeting Maybel mentioned. She had to admit, Jennifer did flirt shamelessly with any man in sight—married or single. But flirting is just flirting, Celeste thought.

"I wonder if the police will question any of the residents here. You know, to see if any of us saw anything or know anything about her." Maybel got up from the couch and stared out the window of Celeste's condo. Certain things weren't very convenient about living at Regal Palms, because of the age of the building, but the view amazed whoever gazed at it. Downtown Sunshine Beach at night lit up like little jewels glowing in the dark sky. Regal Palms also sat a hop, skip, and a jump from the beach. The ocean could be seen from the left of her condo, and the rest of the city to the right. On a clear day, you could catch a glimpse of the Hollywood sign from the rooftop observation deck.

"That would be a lot of people to question," Celeste responded as she stood next to Maybel looking out the window and down at the street. Regal Palms was twelve stories high with three wings to the building, and six units on each floor of each wing. A glorious penthouse that could be accessed from the twelfth floor was perched at the top of the middle wing. Most residents owned their condos, but about a fourth of the residents rented.

"Well, maybe they can just question some of the key residents who have been here since the beginning." Maybel loved reminding everyone she'd lived there since the building was first built.

Celeste smiled at her. "Perhaps you should go back down to the street and offer your services and expertise to them."

Maybel took her seriously and rushed to the door. "Good idea. I'll be back for lunch."

Once alone again, Celeste stood at her window and continued to look down at the street below. She studied what she saw. As a senior insurance claims adjuster, she'd been trained to pay close attention to detail and ask probing questions to obtain insightful answers. Celeste possessed a strong sense of justice and required order in her mind. She knew how to organize fragmented pieces into a full picture, and connecting the dots was her specialty. She observed the crowds of people below and the police cars on the road. Some of the police cars formed a line blocking off traffic. The caffeine from Celeste's coffee hit her brain, and she thought about Jennifer hitting the pavement. Celeste shuddered. She watched Jennifer's body be removed from the street. What a nightmare, she thought. Her inner voice told her something was off, but she wasn't sure what it was.

Chapter Two

A Photographic Memory

Celeste caught up on some of her Saturday chores and cleaned up, paid bills and checked her social media. Most chit chat bored her to death. She wondered what to do for lunch while poking through her fridge. She spotted the bacon. A BLT sounded perfect, and she knew Maybel would like that too. She put several strips of bacon on a roasting pan and popped it in a preheated oven. The house started to smell great. She washed and diced up the tomatoes, toasted bread, and sliced up a few nectarines to have on the side. Maybel loved nectarines.

Unlike Maybel's kitchen, Celeste's had been remodeled. It now included marble counter tops, a farm style sink, beautiful light fixtures and purple barstools at her bar counter. The living room of her condo being small and simple didn't have much furniture; a long white couch and a white furry rug under it. A mid-century style walnut colored wooden coffee table stood in front of the couch, and a giant black and white picture of Sunshine Beach taken back in the 1950's hung over the couch. It made her heart ache to go back in time when she looked at it. One cozy reading chair sat off to the side of the couch: dark grey leather and masculine looking. Along the back east wall of her place, opposite all the windows, were bookshelves. Part of the wall was inset, and she'd hired a handyman to build some custom bookcases she later filled with her favorite authors and unusual nick knacks.

Her place measured only 950 square feet. Other condos in the building were as small as 500 square feet. They built them tiny back in the 1950's. Her place, originally a one bedroom, became a two bedroom after the remodel. Both bedrooms' windows faced to the north. The walls made kind of an octagon shape. One room she used as her bedroom (the one with the bigger closet, of course), and the other bedroom she used as her home office. She hoped her boss would occasionally let her work from home, and he did, but only on the weekends.

The timer for the bacon buzzed, and Celeste took it out of the oven just as Maybel walked back in. "Oh bacon…I love bacon," she said as she took a few deep breaths and down winded the scent of sizzling pork fat. Celeste smiled and put the sandwiches together. She knew Maybel loved to have a cup of coffee with her lunch time sandwich, so she popped a pod into the coffee maker, a nice Italian dark roast. Until Maybel met Celeste, she only drank instant coffee, because that is what George wanted. Since then, Celeste introduced her to other coffees, and they both agreed the Italian dark roast danced the smoothest on their palates.

"Did you get to talk to the police?" Celeste took a bite of her BLT sandwich that dripped with mayonnaise.

Maybel ate a piece of her nectarine first and seemed very thoughtful. Despite her age, Maybel was an attractive lady. Back in a time when gentlemen preferred blonds, her husband George loved his brunette and thought she could give a well know sultry Italian actress a run for her money. A feisty firecracker of a woman, when Maybel went off, she had a tendency to light others' fuses at the same time. "Ya know, there is a detective down there that looks just like Steve McQueen. You're probably too young to know who Steve McQueen is. Anyway, I told him everything I knew about Jennifer. He didn't write any of it down, so he must have one of those photographic memories."

Celeste grinned. "Yes, that must be it, and I do know vaguely who Steve McQueen is."

"You'd like him," Maybel went on, "He's real sexy!"

"Steve McQueen?" Celeste teased.

"No! The hot cop I just spoke to," Maybel said.

Celeste took a deep breath and waived that off in her mind. Celeste was in her early forties, and though she never married or had kids, she'd been engaged twice and traveled 'around the block a few times' as the expression goes. She'd already dated a cop, and the ex before that was a slick insurance salesman who could talk anyone into just about anything. "Do you think we should try to reach out to Jennifer's family?" Celeste asked feeling troubled.

"I think we should," Maybel agreed. "Detective hottie said they already contacted her mother. Imagine getting that call." Maybel and Celeste sat silently finishing their lunch. This wasn't what either of them expected to happen that day.

After lunch, Maybel talked Celeste into walking to the pavilion with her to get some groceries. Celeste used a delivery service for her groceries to save time, along with a laundry service, since she hated using the laundry room in the dingy basement of the building. Celeste suspected that Maybel felt more bothered by this than she let on, so she agreed to go to the store with her. The pavilion next door could be walked to in just a few minutes. It housed the best bakery, a deli that could rival any of the ones in New York, aisles and aisles of specialty items, plus all the regular stuff. A section of fun and seasonal non-food items, with books, blankets and clothes always lured Celeste in. A charming little café inside the store served the best coffee and croissants.

Parking in their neighborhood was tricky. Spots were scarce on the busy street. Lots of people who couldn't find spots would either have to pay for parking in the structure across the street from Regal Palms, or park in the parking lot of the pavilion. If you parked at the pavilion, there was no way to get back out to the street unless you walked through the pavilion. Celeste suspected that is why the Pavilion allowed it knowing it was good for business. You couldn't walk through that pavilion without spending money. Fortunately, Celeste and Maybel didn't need to worry about parking. Maybel because she no longer drove, and Celeste because she had one of the coveted assigned parking spots in Regal Palms under-ground parking structure.

Maybel and Celeste shopped quickly and bought an array of proteins, vegetables, healthy snacks, and beverages. As they walked back home with their groceries, Maybel pointed out the spot on the street where Jennifer landed. Celeste stopped and stared for a moment. She saw the blood spot on the asphalt and shivered. Not the color of blood anymore, but she knew what it had seeped out of. She looked up the length of their building and got dizzy. She really didn't know Jennifer, but she couldn't shake the sick feeling she had about all of this. Celeste wondered why would a young, beautiful girl with her whole life ahead of her kill herself? And in such a brutal manner? Celeste's thoughts wouldn't leave her. "Let's get out of the heat," she quietly said to Maybel.

Chapter Three

The Roof

Celeste put all her groceries away and was doing a bit of food prep for her busy work week when Maybel called her cell phone. "I've been thinking, dear," Maybel whispered, "It might be a good idea if you and I go up to the roof tonight."

"Why? And why are you whispering?" Celeste seldom went up to the rooftop observation deck, even though the view stunned her.

"I just want to scan the area for any clues," Maybel explained.

"Clues?"

"Yeah, clues. Just in case Jennifer didn't commit suicide," Maybel said.

"I'm sure the police already did that," Celeste replied.

Being the self-proclaimed matriarch of the building, Maybel felt a sense of responsibility to look into the situation herself. A mother hen must always protect her little chicks. She said, "Well, of course they did, dear, but they might have missed something."

Celeste thought it would be pointless but had to admit she was a bit curious. She decided to humor Maybel. "Ok, do you want to go up there now?"

"No, we must wait until night fall. I'll meet you out in front of your place at 9 p.m. sharp!"

With a few hours to kill, Celeste finished her food prep, checked her emails and responded to a few friends. Then she painted her fingernails. At 9 p.m., she stepped out into the hallway. Maybel waited for her in a black turtleneck, black pants, and a black ski cap. She held a huge black flashlight in her petite hand. Celeste frowned and asked, "Maybel, what the heck are you wearing?"

"We need to be stealth like, dear. That's why I dressed in all black. The cap and flashlight were George's. Your sweatpants are ok, but that white t-shirt will stick out like a sore thumb. Do you want to go change?"

Celeste walked towards the elevator. "No, I'm good. Let's just go."

They both got in, and Celeste hit the number twelve button to go to the top floor. They rode up in silence. After the elevator dropped them off, they walked towards the end of the hall to the door that led to the tiny stairwell up to the roof. When they got up the steps, they saw yellow caution tape in an X across the door that led out to the roof.

"I don't think we're supposed to go out onto the roof right now," Celeste told Maybel.

"Nonsense, we'll just do what the tape says and be cautious," Maybel reasoned.

Celeste didn't like the idea at all. Maybel opened the door and ducked under the tape. Celeste reluctantly followed her. They stepped out on to the rooftop observation deck. You could hear the hum of the traffic below, and the smell of the salt air felt invigorating. Celeste took in a deep breath. It felt nice to be on the roof again. As she looked out at the city all around her, the summer night air landed a bit warm. The building lights glowed, and the balmy breeze from up high felt pleasant.

"Come on, follow me," Maybel instructed. They walked over to where a set of four wicker chaise lawn chairs were lined up. "I bet this is where she was tanning her ta ta's."

"Do you mean breasts?" Celeste asked.

Maybel nodded. "Yeah, you know those knockers weren't real, right?"

"Why were they called knockers? Is that from the 1950's?" Celeste wondered.

Maybel speculated, "I think they're called knockers because they knock together during all the sex."

Celeste giggled and shook her head.

Maybel moved closer to the lawn chairs. "Dear, control yourself. We're on a recon mission. Here, you shine the flashlight, while I look around." She handed Celeste the heavy flashlight, and Celeste shined it towards the lawn chairs. She knew the police went over everything with a fine-tooth comb, but Maybel poked around anyway. Maybel pulled at something on the back of one of the lawn chairs. "A blond hair. Probably Jennifer's. I guess it would be easy to get your hair caught on the chair. Doesn't really prove anything. Everyone knew she came up here to sun herself all the time. I heard sometimes she even took her top off!"

Celeste's eyes widened. "Where did you hear that from?"

"Don't worry about that now, dear. We have other things we need to focus on," Maybel said and stood up. She looked around the rooftop. Everything appeared to be in order. "Let's walk to the other side, facing Pacific Boulevard."

Celeste followed Maybel to the other end of the roof past the patio area with the fire pit. They both looked over the railing and down at the street. Celeste took a deep calming breath and said, "Dang, that's a long way down."

Maybel replied, "It sure is. When she hit the street, she had her bathing suit on. So, you think she was over on the other side, and then just walked over here and just jumped off?"

"I don't really know what to think, Maybel. It's hard to conceive why someone would do this."

Maybel started to kick her leg up over the railing. "She would have had to have climbed up on this railing to jump off."

"No!" Celeste shouted and pulled Maybel back to her.

"I just wanted to see how hard it would be," Maybel said.

Celeste shook her head and said, "That's not a good idea. You also just put your fingerprints on the railing, but I guess that doesn't matter now. Maybel, I really don't think there is anything else up here for us to see."

At that moment, they heard the door to the roof open. "Come on," Maybel said, and she hurried over to the patio wall and flattened herself against it. Celeste followed. Maybel whispered, "No one is supposed to be up here! Didn't they see the caution tape?"

They waited there against the wall by the penthouse and stayed quiet for a minute. They heard footsteps coming towards them. In the darkness, they saw a man walk over to the railing facing Pacific Boulevard. He looked over it, and then he crouched down and looked around at the ground under the railing. He stood up and walked away. He never saw Celeste or Maybel pressed against the wall.

Celeste whispered, "Do you know who that was?"

"It looked like Tom Fitzpatrick, one of the HOA board members," Maybel said.

"Oh, that makes sense. Maybe he wanted to make sure it is safe up here."

Maybel whispered back, "Or maybe he was returning to the scene of the crime."

"You've been watching too many murder shows," Celeste said. She looked over to her right and saw the side entrance to the penthouse, the one unit that could enter directly out on to the roof without going up the side stairwell. The penthouse included a panoramic view of the roof and the city. "Hey, do you know who lives in the penthouse?" Celeste asked.

"Yeah, it's some rich guy named Billy Cheng and his wife Lily." Maybel straightened out her ski cap. "Rumor has it, he liked watching Jennifer sunbathe, but Lily hated it."

Celeste didn't bother to ask Maybel who she heard that from. She knew she wouldn't get an answer. "Let's get out of here before Billy and Lily see us."

"Well, this was a bust! No pun intended. We didn't find anything," Maybel said as they walked back to the door to the stairwell.

They went back down the stairwell steps and into the hall of the twelfth floor. Celeste felt relieved they didn't get caught. She didn't like breaking rules. When the elevator doors opened, a good looking, muscular Asian man dressed in a three-piece suit stepped out, and a beautiful blond woman followed him. The man gave a slight frown then nodded his head at them, and Celeste figured him to be Billy Cheng. Maybel and Celeste stepped in. After the doors closed, Celeste asked, "Was that Billy and Lily?"

"Yes."

Celeste asked, "She was jealous of Jennifer?" Lily possessed the same blond, buxom look Jennifer Riley had. Billy sure has a type, Celeste thought.

"So I heard, but I don't know why. She's gorgeous. I heard there was one night when they got into a huge fight and were screaming at each about pictures on his phone so loudly someone called the cops on them," Maybel said.

Celeste shook her head. "Drama."

The clunky elevator slowly dropped them back down to the ninth floor. As they walked towards their condos, Maybel said, "Thanks for going up there with me, dear. I appreciate it. I just had to see it for myself." Maybel pulled off the ski cap and fluffed her silver hair.

Celeste asked, "Are you satisfied now?"

"No, not at all. As you know, I've lived here many years, and we've never had anything like this happen. Something doesn't seem right, you know?" Maybel stared at Celeste.

Celeste nodded and knew something wasn't right.

Chapter Four

The Board Meeting

I n the weeks to follow Jennifer's death, things went on as normal. When residents rode the elevator together, they asked each other if they'd heard about the accident. Was it an accident? Celeste wondered. "Horrible, just horrible," everyone mumbled.

Maybel talked Celeste into going to another monthly board meeting. Celeste normally avoided the meetings as she was usually tired after work. Maybel, on the other hand, loved going to them. She treated them like a mixer or an ice cream social, and she even brought cookies and punch. The HOA board meetings were held in the building's small Rec room off the side of the pool. Normally, the only people that attended were the five board members and a handful of people with some sort of grievance they needed to air. This meeting would be standing room only, since everyone heard about Jennifer Riley.

Maybel insisted they get there early to get a good seat. Celeste didn't have time to change out of her work clothes. She had on a black straight skirt, her favorite black wedge heels, and a cream-colored silky frilly blouse with pink and yellow vertical stripes. She'd blown dry her long wavy dark hair that morning. It hung very sleek and shiny. Pink lip gloss still shimmered on her lips. Maybel wore her brown button up the front shirt dress with a white cardigan sweater, and her usual white orthopedic shoes. She'd made chocolate chip cookies, half with walnuts, and half without in case anyone had a nut allergy. After they set out her cookie trays, punch, cups, and napkins, Maybel insisted on greeting all the board members. This amused Celeste, because she knew a few of them didn't like

Maybel and vice versa. The board members were: Vick Arnold—President, Angie Adams—Vice President, Tom Fitzpatrick—Treasurer, Marla Gomez—Secretary.

Celeste sat down to get off her feet. Out of force of habit, she took a seat toward the back of the room. Ever since school, she didn't like sitting in the front rows. Celeste was a bit on the shy side. Tenants trickled in, and before no time, the room buzzed with conversation. Angie and Marla handed out copies of the agenda, but they hadn't printed enough. Celeste and Maybel shared. Celeste put on her glasses to read it. There were basically two categories on the agenda: old business and new business. For the old business, it indicated the board voted to adopt a new mediation process for small claims and past due accounts to avoid going to small claims court. Smart, Celeste thought. The other "old" item indicated the work to repair all the cracks in the pool was done.

There were two items under the new business category. The first one wasn't of much interest to Celeste. They were going to use existing money from the complex's special assessment fund to upgrade the electrical in the laundry room to accommodate two more washers and dryers. Celeste hated the laundry room. It was down in the basement of the under-ground parking structure and always smelled musty. Plus, she didn't like the idea of sharing a washer and dryer with so many other people. Somehow, it didn't seem sanitary. Also, there never seemed to be a free washer or dryer at a good time. Furthermore, some people were very inconsiderate and would leave their clothes in the washer or dryer long after their cycles were done. For these reasons, Celeste did not use the laundry room in the building. I'll stick with my outside laundry service thank you very much, she thought. The second item under new business on the agenda perked her interest. It mentioned the possibility of installing security cameras on the roof.

Obviously, this came up due to what happened with Jennifer. There were already security cameras in the lobby and at the outside front entrance of the building, but it had never been discussed to put them on the roof before. Lots of tenants hung out on the roof. The amazing view and patio with a fire pit made it appealing. Plus, there was a high-grade telescope up there. They would have to charge every tenant a one-time special assessment fee of $75 to be able to add security cameras to the roof and stairwell. While this didn't seem too bad, Celeste was sure there would be a lot of grumbling over it. Most condo owners in the complex didn't like to pay any more above and beyond their monthly HOA dues for anything.

The meeting began on time and started with Vick Arnold the president of the HOA board hitting a little gavel on the table. All four members sat at the front of the room at a long rectangle table, really giving them a sense of self-importance. Maybel leaned towards Celeste and whispered, "What an ego maniac. He says I'm the ego maniac, but *he's* the ego maniac! Vick's ego is so big it takes up this whole room! I'm surprised the rest of us were able to fit in here!"

Vick Arnold hit the gavel on the table multiple times, and after much abuse to his mighty gavel, he shouted, "Attention everyone! Attention!" Vick commanded the room to be silent. Celeste looked around and noticed a full house. She saw a man standing against the wall off to the side, behind the cookie table, wearing an outdated tweed sports coat, a white dress shirt, and khaki pants. He shoved a cookie in his mouth and chomped on it. She wondered if he was the detective Maybel referred to. He looked like the type of man women often said yes to.

Detective Brian Bahn started out as a beat cop twenty years earlier, played his cards right, kept his nose clean, kissed a little ass, and made detective. Bahn was tough and didn't believe in exfoliating, but he did believe in manscaping. Twice divorced with no kids, he now roamed the dating scene like a hungry lion out on the prowl. He was a lover and a fighter but a fighter first. He felt good fighting skills made him a better lover, and he asked for forgiveness of his sins in advance. As he leaned back against the wall of the Regal Palms Rec room, he wondered if he should eat another cookie. He sipped his punch and watched the room carefully.

"This meeting will come to order," Vick shouted. The conversations in the room quickly died out. He kept banging the gavel until it did. Celeste really wasn't too interested in all of this and was tired from a long day at work that for her started at 4 a.m. that morning. She took her glasses back off, closed her eyes and tried to concentrate on what was being said. When she opened her eyes, she noticed the guy leaning against the wall staring at her. He looked away quickly. Vick went on and on about the old business giving everyone an update on the new procedures and repairs to the pool. He asked if there were any questions to those items. Alice Parker, one of Maybel's friends and part of Maybel's weekly poker club, asked a question about the pool usage and if the hours could be extended. Vick barked, "Absolutely not! Those hours are in place for everyone's safety and to keep the noise down late at night."

Alice protested, "Those hours aren't about safety. It's just as safe to swim in the evening as it is in the morning."

"I also said it's to keep the noise down at night!" Vick retorted.

Maybel leaned over to Celeste and asked, "Who died and made Vick boss? Like it would kill them to leave the pool open a little later. You got to be kind to the people, you know? I was always for the people, not the power."

Celeste nodded.

After Vick shut Alice down, he went on to the new business. He talked in painful detail about the laundry room upgrades that would be done. Alex Graham jumped up and shouted, "It's about time." Celeste turned to look at him. Alex, her short little neighbor that rented the unit next to hers, sat down next to her before the meeting started. Maybel thought Celeste should date him, but Maybel thought any single man was someone Celeste should date.

Maybe because Maybel was from a different generation, but she just didn't get that Celeste was content with her life and made her career a priority. Celeste didn't let it bother her, because she knew it came from a place of love.

Vick gave Alex a dirty look and said, "The board acknowledges that this was a project that should have been addressed a while ago. However, there was not enough money to cover it in the special assessment fund until now." Alex sunk back down on his chair and disappeared.

Mark Summons, another tenant who lived on the third floor next to Jennifer's condo, put his hand up and spoke. "Yes, I for one am very glad that the board has finally decided to upgrade the electrical and add more washers and dryers. There simply aren't enough for a building this large. I can't tell you how many times I've been doing my laundry and had to turn someone away." Mark puffed out his chest in a way Celeste found to be ridiculous. He smelled faintly of body odor and seemed like a creep to her.

Tom Fitzpatrick, another board member asked, "Do you have a question, Mark?"

"No, I just wanted to make that point," Mark said and cycled back down to his chair.

There were more hands up with questions about the laundry room and complaints about how inconsiderate others were. Celeste's mind wandered. She thought about all the things she needed to take care of the next day at work…so many insurance claims to be adjusted. Again, when she looked up, she noticed the man against the wall staring at her, and when she made eye contact with him, he quickly looked away. Finally, Vick got to the last item on the agenda. "Now ladies and gentlemen, as you all know, Jennifer Riley died a few weeks ago. We are not entirely sure of the circumstances, and we think she may have jumped off the roof. It was a horrible tragedy, and due to this event, we think we need to make another change to our security system. Detective Brian Bahn of the Sunshine Beach police brought this to our attention when he came out the day of the incident to investigate. It was his recommendation that we add security cameras to the roof. If we were to do this, we would need to charge every owner a one-time special assessment fee of $75 to cover all the expenses associated with the upgrade."

Grumbling rumbled through the old dingy Rec room. Celeste heard someone in front of her say, "But I thought Jennifer committed suicide. Why would this be a security issue that has to cost us money?" Vick frowned and said that Detective Bahn would answer any questions as to why this would be needed. Vick extended his hand towards the side of the room where Detective Bahn stood with his back against the wall.

Maybel whispered in Celeste's ear, "That's the super sexy detective I was telling you about."

Detective Bahn (pronounced BANE as Maybel explained to Celeste earlier) gave a wave hello to the room. Celeste thought he seemed arrogant and decided she didn't like him. He addressed the room with authority, and a clearing of his throat, before he spoke in a deep voice. "Ladies and gentlemen, while I can't discuss all the details of an ongoing investigation, I will say that it would be helpful to all of you to have increased security on the roof. If the building had had security cameras on the roof, we would have known exactly what happened to Jennifer Riley. This really is for everyone's protection."

Muffled conversations streamed all around. Vick spoke up again, "The Board has the right to charge one-time assessment fees once a year, as long as it is not more than five percent of the annual HOA dues. It's in the by-laws. This would fall under that guideline. We don't need tenant approval." With that, more questions and discussion came about.

Billy Cheng stood in the back of the room wearing his navy blue power suit with his hair slicked back. "I know I for one would be happy to pay the one-time fee for extra security."

Maybel leaned towards Celeste and whispered, "Well, that's because Mr. Moneybags in the penthouse can afford it. I'm on a fixed income."

Once the meeting concluded, Maybel dragged Celeste over to Detective Bahn. "Detective Bahn, this is my friend and neighbor Celeste Ravenna." Maybel waived her hand towards Celeste.

Detective Brian Bahn wasn't shy, and his eyes wandered all over Celeste. He instantly trusted her and let his guard down, but Celeste never trusted anyone. Looking at her reminded him of a woman in a Botticelli painting enveloped by angels. He knew he wanted his body close to hers. He extended his callused hand to Celeste, and she politely shook it. He held her hand longer than he needed to. He intonated, "Ravenna?"

"Yes, like the city in Italy," Celeste replied realizing when she took her hand back, Detective Bahn got cookie crumbs on it. When he spoke, she also noticed his tongue was bright red from the punch he'd been drinking.

"Sounds like they named a city after your beautiful raven-colored hair," he said, and his eyes stayed on her.

She took her hand back and almost blushed, almost. Celeste would not fall for some fake charm or clever line. She quickly changed the subject and said with certainty, "If you're recommending the complex put in security cameras on the roof, you must not think it was a suicide."

A cocky smiled formed on his face, and he looked like the cat that swallowed the canary. Celeste was bright and no nonsense. "Those are details I can't go into, but I will say you should be very careful if you go up to the roof. Don't go alone."

Celeste frowned and said, "So there was definitely foul play."

"Miss Riley may have had an enemy," he continued, "Maybel here was kind enough to tell me of Jennifer's wanton ways. We're looking into a few things." Celeste looked over at Maybel, who grinned from ear to ear at Detective Bahn as she nodded her head.

At that moment, several other tenants came up to Detective Bahn to ask questions including Vick Arnold, who greeted Detective Bahn like an old friend. Vick always wanted to be a cop, but since he couldn't pass the psych evaluation, he had to settle for being a security guard. He instantly looked up to Detective Bahn and quickly befriended him on the day of Jennifer's death. Detective Bahn possessed enough of an ego to be flattered by this. As president of the HOA board, Vick was also Detective Bahn's point of contact at Regal Palms. Vick wanted to faithfully help Detective Bahn in any way he could. He wondered if he helped enough, if he could get some sort of honorable mention in the news. Vick excitedly jammed his body between Detective Bahn and Maybel so he could speak to him. When he did, Maybel said, "Excuse me Vick, but we were speaking with Detective Bahn first! You don't get to push ahead of us just because you are the current sitting president! If you were a better leader, perhaps none of this would have even happened!"

Vick scolded her, "Maybel, we don't have time for your idle gossip. Why don't you go knit yourself a scarf or a hat or a muzzle—anything that covers your mouth."

Maybel bristled and snapped back, "You're not going to silence me, Vick! You are the most corrupt president Regal Palms has ever had! We're going to recall you!"

"No other president has done more than I have for this building," Vick bragged proudly, and he reminded Celeste of a well-known republican who also liked to brag about his presidency.

Steam came out of Maybel's ears. "Vick, you don't even own your own place! You rent from your daddy! You are an illegitimate president, and you know it!"

Celeste took this as her cue to walk away. "Ok, I'm leaving," she said to Maybel.

"But my cookie trays," Maybel responded.

"You don't have to leave just because I'm leaving. You can stay and chat with everyone," Celeste said and walked out of the Rec room.

As she did, she could have sworn she heard Vick invite Detective Bahn to the annual Regal Palms Halloween party which was still two months away. "I've even got a great costume idea we could try!" Vick said excitedly.

Celeste got to the elevator quickly, hit the up button and waited. Maybel was hot on her heels and got in the elevator with her. "Oh boy, Detective Bahn looked at you like you were a ribeye steak, and he hadn't eaten in two weeks!"

"Maybel," Celeste said and shook her head.

"He really likes you. You could do a lot worse than a successful, handsome detective."

"He's arrogant," Celeste replied.

Maybel retorted, "Well, sometimes so are you."

Celeste laughed and stayed silent as they rode up to the ninth floor. Maybel continued to talk about Detective Bahn's attributes, but Celeste tuned it out. She felt a bit disturbed by the warning Detective Bahn gave her not to go up to the roof by herself… a warning she knew shouldn't be ignored.

Chapter Five

The Street Festival

In the days to follow the board meeting and the eerie warning Detective Brian Bahn gave Celeste, she tried to put the whole thing out of her mind. The first Saturday after the meeting, she decided instead of fixing lunch for Maybel and herself, she would buy Maybel lunch. That weekend an annual summer arts festival was going on about two blocks over from their street, on Lansing Street in the east village. Regal Palms was a hop, skip, and a jump from the historical arts district in Sunshine Beach. They blocked off a few roads for it and sold lots of street food, arts, crafts, and clothes. Loud bands played fast music, and colorful booths were set up for face painting. Temporary, rickety rides were erected for the festival that always seemed unsafe to Celeste.

Normally, Celeste would have preferred to stay home, but something made her want to get out of the building that day. With a hot day ahead of her, she stood in front of her closet and tried to pick out an outfit. A few pairs of shorts she hadn't worn in years stared back at her. "Nope, I'm too old to wear those now," she said to herself. She decided on a lightweight white V neck t-shirt and a pair of burgundy Capri pants. Since they'd be walking a lot, she grabbed her most comfortable pair of tennis shoes and put her hair up in a high ponytail. That would help with the heat, she thought. She brushed on some metallic gold eyeshadow, thickened her eyelashes with mascara, and stained her lips with a burgundy matte lipstick. After Maybel rang her doorbell, Celeste asked, "How about we go to the art festival on Lansing Street?"

Maybel's eyes lit up. "Ok! Good thing I wore my walking shoes," Maybel stuck out her foot and pointed to her white orthopedic footwear. That day, Maybel wore white polyester pants and a pink floral print shirt.

Celeste waited until they got outside the elevator in the lobby before putting on her Jackie-O sunglasses. When they hit the pavement outside, it felt hotter than Celeste thought it would. The humid summer air stuck to her. She took a deep breath and decided to grin and bear it. They walked half a block north and then two blocks east over to the festival chatting along the way. Maybel asked about Celeste's work, and Celeste gave her a brief update. Celeste felt her work wasn't that interesting to people outside the insurance industry, and she didn't want to bore people with too many details.

When they approached Lansing Street, they spotted a huge crowd already at the festival. The streets were full of food booths serving hot dogs, hamburgers, tacos, submarine sandwiches and kabobs grilled on a smokey charcoal BBQ. There were plenty of things to drink like tart lemonade, fruity iced tea, bubbly sodas, dark beer, sparkling wine and icy margaritas. Dessert booths were set up and sold cinnamon dusted churros, ice cream with sprinkles, twisty fried funnel cakes, chunky cookies and cupcakes with frosting piled three inches high. Somewhere in the festival they were making cotton candy too, and Celeste knew this because she could smell the warm spun sugar in the hot summer air. She breathed in the sweetness.

They passed all the booths that sold clothes first. Maybel found a hat she liked; a big white straw hat with a pretty pink rose on it. Sold. She put it on at the festival. Next, they made their way past the jewelry booths as heat radiated up off the asphalt. Beautifully beaded necklaces and earrings dangled from display hooks. It looked like a hippie's paradise. One man's booth housed some handmade bracelets he fashioned out of silver spoons. He masterfully bent and twisted his wares around to make circles and connect them together. Celeste admired the craftmanship of the delightful dining ware cuffs and slipped one on. While they were unusual and interesting, she was hardly born with a silver spoon in her mouth, let alone on her wrist. It would probably clunk around too much on her keyboard when she typed, she thought. She slipped the bracelet off her slim wrist and put it back.

They made their way over to the food section and ordered fish and chips with iced tea and lots of lemon on the side. When Celeste asked for some malt vinegar to go with her fish and chips, the man gave her a disgusted look. What was the big deal? She thought tartar sauce was gross. Warm mayonnaise on a hot day—no thank you! He tossed a few packets of the vinegar her way without looking at her and quickly turned to help the next customer. She carried the tray of food and drinks over to one of the small plastic tables in the eating area. A few chairs were open, and Celeste and Maybel sat down, feeling lucky they got just a little bit of shade on that brutal summer day. The white flimsy plastic chair felt like it was going to give way under Celeste. She tried to hold still while she ate her lunch.

It wasn't the healthiest lunch, but Celeste figured all the extra walking would burn off the grease. She enjoyed the salty food and was glad she had a cold iced tea to wash it down. They ate in silence taking in the festival around them. In the distance, they could hear a band playing some sort of 80's song, but Celeste wasn't sure which one. The duet lyrics sang of a man telling his woman he'd made her who she was, and the woman sang back, adamantly denying it and claiming her independence. Crowds of people walked around eating food on sticks, shopping for light weight summer garb, dancing, drinking, and in some cases drunk dancing.

As Celeste wiped her oily hands off on a paper napkin, she spotted Vick Arnold and Tom Fitzpatrick headed their way. She nodded her head towards them, and Maybel turned to look.

"Oh God! It's that dim wit," she said with a disgusted look on her face. Celeste smiled. She found it funny how much Vick got on Maybel's nerves.

"Hello ladies," Tom said greeting them with a chipper smile. "It's nice to see you here. Are you enjoying the festival?"

"The fish and chips are great. Have you eaten anything yet?" Celeste asked.

Tom rubbed his stomach with one hand and said, "I can feel the heart burn coming on from the chili fries." Tom stood almost as tall as Vick but didn't have the pot belly Vick had.

Celeste asked, "Vick, how about you?"

"Corn dog," Vick replied. He acted as if it was an inconvenience to answer, but the truth was he absolutely loved his American hot dog dipped in a high caloric cornmeal batter, deep fat fried to a golden-brown perfection, and slathered with mustard. He even chewed the crispy bits off the stick before throwing the stick in the trash.

Maybel verbally poked at Vick saying, "I'm surprised to see you without your gavel."

Vick quickly retorted, "I'm surprised to see you minding your own business for once."

Maybel grunted.

"Well, we hate to eat and run, but I'm dying to check out all the artwork," Celeste said and stood up. She didn't like tension and wanted to move on.

Tom bowed his head at them as a goodbye.

Celeste and Maybel pushed through the crowds of sunny faced Californians and made their way over to the art booths. They looked through watercolors of oceans and mountains, pastels of beautiful flowers and butterflies, sculptures of busts and wild animals, portraits of strangers with soulful eyes, ceramics for the home, charcoal drawings of symbols and dragons, and other handmade items. A fringy, plumed and netted handmade dream catcher with light fluffy purple feathers caught Celeste's eye. She thought of all the beautiful dreams she could dream under its spell and decided to purchase it.

After perusing all the art booths, Maybel asked her if she wanted to go on one of the rides. Celeste didn't, but since it seemed like Maybel did, she agreed. They pushed and shimmied through more crowds of people and made their way across the street to the rides. There was a merry-go-round for the kids, a Ferris wheel, a small loopy rickety looking roller coaster, and some bumpy bumper cars bouncing around. Fortunately, Maybel wanted to go on the Ferris wheel. "Good choice," Celeste praised her. They got in line with everyone else and waited in the hot sun. Maybel's new hat shielded her scalp from the blazing summer sunshine.

"Did you know Tom was in the military?" Maybel asked.

"No, I didn't. But that doesn't surprise me. He seems like the type."

"Yeah, he served in Afghanistan and was injured in the line of duty. He has some sort of nerve damage in his arm…can barely use it now," Maybel said.

"Aw, that's too bad. He's such a nice guy," Celeste said.

Maybel snorted and replied, "Yeah, a lot nicer than Vick. I don't know why he's palling around with that dipstick."

While they waited in line, Celeste spotted Billy Cheng and his wife Lily. His greased back hair glistened in the sun, and he wore a red Hawaiian print shirt, white shorts and some sort of sandals. His wife Lily draped her curvy body in a hot pink halter style sun dress that had no back to it. The front of the dress was cut down to her belly button. She also wore what some might call "stripper heels". Celeste didn't know how she could walk around in those. If she had them on her feet, she'd break an ankle within the first two minutes.

Maybel stared at Lily's bare back and said, "I hope she's wearing sunscreen."

Celeste couldn't help but notice it sounded like they were arguing. Lily threw her hands up in the air and looked exasperated. "Well, what do you want me to do then?!" She shouted at him. Billy responded to her, but Celeste couldn't tell what he said. Celeste continued to watch them behind her dark sunglasses. Lily started to walk away from him, and he grabbed her arm yanking her back, quite forcefully. Lily looked scared. He pointed his finger in her face. "Don't park in that place again. I told you the car isn't safe there." Billy shook Lily a little. It looked like he tried to shake some sense into her. Celeste felt sorry for her. She wasn't sure what they were really fighting about, but whatever it was, Billy didn't need to get so rough with her. Lily nodded her head at him, and he let go of her.

Celeste frowned. Maybel leaned into her and said, "You know, he bought her a brand new BMW. They've only got one reserved spot in our parking structure, so he makes her park across the street while he parks his Porsche in the underground structure. What a D bag, huh?"

"D bag?" Celeste asked.

"It means douc-"

"No! No, no. I know what it means. I was just surprised to hear you say it," Celeste said cutting Maybel off from explaining.

Maybel looked quite proud of herself. "I'm hip to what the young kids say."

They got on the Ferris wheel, and it too had a wobbly seat that felt like it would give way. Celeste held her breath and remained still until it stopped rocking. They continued to load other folks on, and once everyone was on it, they did a good go around. Celeste loved the view from up high. The volume on the city turned down for a few fleeting seconds when they rode to the top. She even felt a little cool breeze blow through her hair. Maybel laughed and held onto her hat.

After the Ferris wheel, they fought the crowds of sweaty people on the way out but stopped at the ice cream booth, a chocolate gelato for Maybel and raspberry sorbet for Celeste. They ate their frozen treats out of plastic bowls with small plastic spoons and slowly walked back home.

"You know, Maybel, I was thinking. You mentioned it was rumored that Billy Cheng was involved somehow with Jennifer Riley. Today we saw he has a bit of a temper. Do you think it could be possible that Billy was afraid Lily would find out about Jennifer, and Billy pushed Jennifer off the roof?"

Maybel thought about this for a minute before responding, "Well, I guess that's possible, dear. But my money is on Vick. It was also rumored that Vick was sniffing around Jennifer too. If anyone would push someone off the roof, it would be Vick! He's such an A hole! Jennifer probably spurned Vick's obscene advances, and then that gigantic ego of his couldn't handle it!"

Celeste pondered these two suspects, the latter seeming unlikely to her. She felt thankful to be in the air conditioning once they got back in the lobby of their building. They waited for what felt like forever for the elevator. Once inside her condo, Celeste undressed and hopped in the shower. She kept the water cold to cool off and wash the sticky day away. Then, she got into a lightweight night shirt. No sense in putting real clothes back on. She curled up in her leather chair and read for a few hours.

Later that night when she felt hungry again, she poked around in her refrigerator to find something to eat. She found the fixings for a chef salad and was glad she wouldn't have to run her oven on a hot day. She shredded the cold crisp lettuce and diced up all the other ingredients. She tossed it all in a creamy dressing and sat down. She didn't know why, but sometimes, especially on a hot day, she craved iceberg lettuce. Kind of a strange thing to crave, she thought to herself.

Once done with her salad, she got up and cleaned her kitchen. She washed dishes, scoured the sink, put dishes away, wiped off the counters and swept the floor. The trash can over flowed, so it was time to empty it. She threw on her robe out of modesty and grabbed her trash bag. She went out of her condo and down the hall to the trash shoot. She quickly stuffed her bag down the smelly trash shoot and headed back before anyone would see her in her pajamas. But just as she passed the elevator, it dinged.

Alex Graham jumped out. "Celeste, nice to see you," he chirped.

"Alex, hi!" Celeste noticed the bags in his hands were from the art festival and asked, "Did you just come from the art festival?"

"Yeah, I got a couple of small pictures to hang on my walls and some Baklava from the Greek booth. Did you go to the festival? Are you sick? Is that why you are in your pajamas so early on a Saturday night?"

Celeste felt slightly embarrassed. She tightened the robe around herself and explained, "Yeah, we went to the festival too. It was so hot out when I came back home, I took a shower and just got into my P.J.'s to cool off. That Baklava sounds yummy! I bought a dream catcher, and I plan on putting it to good use. Good night." She waved and walked quickly back to her place.

He waved and his voice trailed behind her, "Sweet dreams…"

Chapter Six

The Pool

Celeste arrived the next Thursday night at Maybel's place for their standing dinner date and could smell beef sizzling. "I'm making ribeyes," Maybel said smiling. For a second, Celeste remembered what Maybel said about Detective Bahn and wondered if that was why Maybel was making them. "We're also having salad and mashed potatoes. It's almost ready." Celeste asked if she could help, but Maybel never really let her help much. Cooking for family and friends was Maybel's love language.

Maybel's place had not been upgraded like Celeste's. While it was old, it was well kept and perfectly clean. She had a nice view of the north side of the city. Years ago, when her and George bought their co-op, they couldn't afford the pricier units that faced the ocean. In the years to follow, high rise buildings were put up and blocked most tenants view of the ocean on the south side. As the president of the board, Maybel fought the good fight with the city, but lost. Vick never would have done that for Regal Palms, she thought to herself. Vick would have encouraged the industrial building saying it would be good for the city's economy, not caring at all about the little guy.

During dinner, Maybel let Celeste know she ran into Jennifer Riley's mother when her mother showed up at Jennifer's condo to go through her things to pack up. Celeste asked, "How did you just happen to run into her? We're on the ninth floor, and Jennifer's place is on the third floor. What were you doing on the third floor?"

"Don't worry about that. That doesn't matter. The point is, while I was talking to the poor woman, she mentioned how this didn't make any sense. Apparently, Jennifer had just gotten engaged and was really excited. Her mother didn't know who the man was, but Jennifer promised her mother she would introduce them soon," Maybel said.

Celeste agreed that was strange. "Well Detective Bahn practically said it wasn't safe to go on the roof, so something is up. And what girl gets engaged and then kills herself? Unless…maybe the engagement had been called off?"

Maybel shook her head and said, "No, her mother said she spoke with Jennifer the day before she died. We probably shouldn't go up to the roof by ourselves. By the way, Alice wants to have a pool party this Saturday." Maybel looked at Celeste and waited for a response.

Celeste stalled for time by chewing her steak. "A pool party?"

"Yes, since the pool had been closed down for so long, and it's the end of summer, she thought it would be fun to have a pool party," Maybel explained.

The pool was a tiny rectangle with two patio tables off to the side of it and a few rickety chairs. It wasn't much of anything, and it backed up against a brick wall. Celeste had no intention of going out in public in bathing suit either at this time in her life, but she knew Alice loved to swim. "I'll bring the drinks," Celeste said. What the hell, she thought, I don't have to actually go swimming.

Maybel looked so happy. "Wonderful! I'll let Alice know. She wanted us to gather around 4 p.m. so we have enough time to have some snacks, chat for a while and then take an evening swim."

When Saturday rolled around, Maybel and Celeste decided to forgo their normal lunch date since they'd be seeing each other down at the pool later that day. Celeste put on a butter yellow summer sun dress, a floppy yellow hat and some sandals. This is as festive as I am going to get, she thought. She mixed up a big, strong pitcher of margaritas with tequila, Cointreau and lime juice. Maybel said she'd bring the chips and salsa, and they met up by the elevator around 3:45 p.m. Maybel didn't like to be late, and you never knew how long the creaky elevator would take in a large building like theirs.

Once by the pool, Celeste was surprised to see only one family swimming in it. It was 90°F out, but since they were so close to the beach, a breeze fluttered through the summer air. She set out her pitcher of iced margaritas, the limes, salt and the cups. Fortunately, the two tables were under umbrellas. Celeste sat down in the shade, but beads of sweat were already forming across her nose. Since she was in the shade, she took off her hat which seemed to only serve to make her head hotter. Alice and Janet arrived right after Celeste and Maybel. Janet brought brownies, and Alice brought some little sandwiches.

Janet and Alice were both in Maybel's weekly poker club and knew each other for years. They were long-time residents of Regal Palms—Alice owned, and Janet rented. Celeste got a kick out of them. They told the funniest stories and had the best outlook on life. She poured margaritas and tried not to think about the heat. She offered drinks to the other three, and they all accepted. Janet was a retired teacher and loved to correct everyone's grammar. Her husband John kept to himself, so Celeste didn't know much about him. Alice was a retired postal worker and a widow like Maybel. She reminded Celeste of Ethel Merman, not just in looks, but in her speech patterns and the sound of her voice.

Alice looked Celeste square in the eye and asked her, "Celeste, what do you think really happened to Jennifer?"

Celeste paused before she spoke. The first margarita was already making her head fuzzy on an empty stomach. "I think a jilted lover tossed her off the roof."

Alice and Janet's eyes widened. "That's what we think too," Alice continued, "I mean, why else would we need to put cameras up there? We've lived here for years and never needed cameras up there. But which jealous lover? It was rumored she had several." Alice was part of Maybel's phone tree.

As they continued to discuss the situation, Maybel started to reminisce a little. Maybe it was the alcohol talking, but Celeste noticed Maybel was in rare form with her story telling. "One time, Jennifer had walked into the lobby with a few bags of groceries. This was back when George was still alive. God rest his soul. We just got back from a doctor's appointment when we ran into Jennifer. Well, you know, George could never resist talking to a pretty lady, and he offered to help carry her groceries. She gladly handed all her bags over to him, and when he started to walk to the elevator, she said to him 'Oh no I *neeeeeeever* take the elevator. I always take the stairs. It's good exercise'. So, George wanting to impress her, carried all her groceries up three flights of stairs. When he got back to our place, he huffed and puffed on wobbly knees. He was so exhausted he took a four-hour nap! That man never once helped me carry our groceries," Maybel said.

"Jennifer seemed to have that effect on men," Janet mused. Celeste noticed she was frowning.

"Well, yes, but George always did have his brains in his pants," Maybel said, looked at Celeste, and then whispered to her, "That means he let his penis guide him."

Celeste laughed and said, "Yeah, got it." Maybel was under the false impression that since Celeste was not married, she was sexually naïve.

"Then, that night," Maybel continued, "Celeste, cover your ears. George was so aroused he wanted to make whoopie in the bathtub. The bathtub! Well, I won't go into all the details, but let me just say it didn't go smoothly. He scratched his ass on the bathtub faucet, sloshed water all over the floor, and ruined my best bathroom rug." Laughter from the ladies all around—even Celeste, who though she put her hands over her ears, still heard the whole story.

Alice shared a story of when she needed to do her laundry right after Jennifer. "I found an item of clothing of hers left in the dryer. It was so small I thought it was a red shoestring," Alice said chuckling.

Janet asked, "Was it one of those thong underwear?"

"Butt floss," Maybel called it.

Alice kept laughing. "Yeah, I had never seen panties so small before. I don't know how those could have been comfortable. Jennifer came back into the laundry room looking for it, and she even had the nerve to act like I took it on purpose. What the heck would I have done with it!?"

"Well, maybe now it won't be so bad that they're adding a couple of extra washers and dryers in the laundry room," Janet added.

"But that won't keep folks from leaving their skanky undies behind," Maybel said sipping her second margarita. She explained to Celeste, "You see, Celeste, some women like to lure men in with lingerie, and Jennifer was one of those women. God rest her soul."

The four of them sat there for a long time talking, drinking, eating, exchanging building stories until Vick Arnold showed up. His tall frame cast a shadow on their patio table. He barked, "Ladies, remember the pool closes at 9 p.m. sharp!"

"Vick, it's only 7 p.m.," Maybel said not concerned about his warning.

"I'm aware of the time, Maybel. I have a watch, and I don't need you to tell me what time it is! I know the pool just newly reopened, but you all must still abide by the curfew," he commanded and walked off.

When he was out of earshot, Maybel said, "He is such a little prick!"

"That's why he's called Vick the prick," Alice said.

"I may have started that nickname. You know, when I was the board president, I never cared about the pool hours. All that mattered was that the residents had fun and were safe. He's such a control freak!" Maybel shook her head.

Celeste stuck around a bit longer before bowing out. Alice wanted to stay for a while and take a swim before the pool closed. In her early years, Alice swam on a synchronized swimming team. Her home movies showed her moving around in the water like a mermaid. Celeste and the rest of them watched them once. Now that she was older, she didn't swim as often, but her arthritis drove her back into the pool on occasion.

"Goodnight, ladies," Celeste said as she stood up and grabbed her pitcher. "It's been fun, but I'm going to head back up to my place, do some reading and catch up on my sleep."

Maybel looked at Janet and Alice and asked, "Can you believe this beautiful young lady is going to turn in at 7 p.m. on a Saturday night?"

Celeste curtsied and got the heck out of there before they bugged her to go swimming. Once inside her condo, she changed into her jammies, got into bed and started reading a good book. She fell asleep a couple of hours later and dreamt she was a synchronized swimmer. She stood under a waterfall in a pretty, white bathing suit. In the dream, Maybel, Alice and Janet all swam along side her in perfect synchronicity. Unfortunately, the dream catcher she bought at the art festival didn't work that night…

Alice

Well, if the other ladies don't want to go swimming, then that is their loss, Alice Parker thought to herself. She stood up, stepped out of her flip flops, and took off her swim cover-up. She carefully folded it and put it in the big straw beach bag she brought down with her. She reached around in the bag and found her swim cap. It was the one she'd worn for many years back when she did synchronized swimming; a light pink with bright yellow flowers on it. Alice loved that swim cap. It reminded her of a time when she was much more active. She gingerly put it on her head and made sure her hair was tucked into it. She could smell the old latex it was made from.

She walked over to the pool, grabbed the railings, and held onto them tightly as she carefully descended the steps leading into the shallow end. In the old days, Alice would have swan dived into the pool, but now, she wasn't brave enough to do that. Her back gave her trouble most days and so did the arthritis in her knees. The water felt good as she submerged the lower half of her body into the tepid pool. While in the shallow end, she walked around and twisted the upper half of her body to warm up.

Alice bent her knees, so that the water came up to right below her chin. She waded around in it, feeling buoyant and light as a feather. Acclimated to the water, Alice swam the breaststroke to the deep end. She tapped the edge of the deep end, flipped around, and swam back to the shallow end. Her aging body remembered this, and though she wasn't as fast as she used to be, she still swam with expertise. She did a few laps, tuning out the rest of the world while she swam. When back in the shallow end, she did some of her old moves. She submerged herself under water holding her breath. She could hold her breath a long time too. She went down to the bottom of the shallow end and touched the floor of the pool. They did fix all the cracks, she thought to herself. She did a couple of underwater summer salts of joy.

As Alice tried to swim back up to the top of the water, she felt pressure on her head. She tried to pull away from it, but she wasn't strong enough. She felt a hand on her shoulder. Alice and her murderer squared off in the triangle shaped pool. She thrashed around frantically, and her feet and knees scraped the bottom of the pool. She could not get her head above water no matter how hard she tried. With all the O2 ready to burst out of her, she fought as long as she could. The pool waited patiently for her. Then suddenly, she tasted chlorine in her mouth. H2O invaded and seized her lungs.

Minutes later, Alice's lifeless body gently floated to the top of the pool.

Chapter Seven

It Remains to Be Seen

The Sunday morning after the pool party, Celeste wanted to go shopping. After a cup of coffee, she jumped in the shower. She let her hair air dry, which meant it ended up somewhere between wavy and curly. She put on a pair of electric blue tapered Capri pants and an electric blue and red plaid flannel shirt. She wasn't afraid of color. After applying plenty of mascara and bright red lipstick, she donned on her red wedge heels and tied a red bandana around her head as a head band, rockabilly style.

As she started to make a protein shake, she heard an abrupt knock at her door. By the sound, she knew it wasn't Maybel. The peek hole revealed Detective Bahn. What the hell is he doing here, she wondered. For a second, she contemplated not opening the door, but she knew she had to. "Detective Bahn, nice to see you again," she said and kept her tone polite and her hand on the door.

"I need to ask you some questions. May I come in?" he asked. She looked down and saw he held some type of sandwich in a little paper bag from the pavilion next door.

She reluctantly stepped aside and waved her hand towards her living room. "Sure." As he brushed past her, she could smell his cologne. Normally, she didn't like the smell of colognes or perfumes, but he smelled quite clean.

Detective Brian Bahn walked in and quickly assessed Celeste's place. She clearly made a decent amount of money and possessed good taste. He moved towards the west wall of windows and exclaimed, "Wow! What a view!"

"Yeah, that's what made me buy this place," Celeste said and smiled. She pointed to his bag. "Normally I would offer you something to eat, but I see you already have something."

He held up his sandwich and said, "Oh yeah, this is an artesian breakfast sandwich I got at the café in the pavilion. There wasn't any parking on the street, so I had to park over there in their lot. I hope you don't mind if I eat while we talk. I was up all night working on a homicide, and I haven't eaten since yesterday afternoon."

"Please don't wait on my account. Have a seat," she said and motioned to the grey leather chair. He sat down and sprawled out, taking up the whole chair. Celeste sat on the couch but not too close. She landed somewhere in the middle of the couch and turned her body to face him. He took a bite of his sandwich. She waited while he chewed and wondered how long it was going to be.

As he chewed, Detective Bahn closed his eyes, threw his head back a little, and made a moaning sound indicating his delight over the breakfast sandwich. "Oh man," he said with his mouth still full, "This sandwich is so good. The bacon is so smoky. Do you like smoky bacon?"

Celeste side eyed him and his sandwich when he dropped a piece of something on his lap, picked it up, and popped it into his mouth. "Uh…yeah, sure. Do you want a cup of coffee to go with it? Or do you want a napkin?" Celeste asked.

"Nah, I'm good," he said and took another big bite of the egg sandwich. He bit right into the runny yolk. This led to egg yolk running down his hand, and he licked it off the side of his palm.

Celeste flinched and said, "I really feel like I need to get you a napkin." She jumped up and headed towards her kitchen. She clawed at a paper towel and ripped it off. Ugh gawd he's going to get yolk all over my leather chair, she thought. She folded it neatly as she walked back towards him. "Here you go," she said and smiled stiffly.

As he ate, Detective Bahn looked at Celeste and assessed her. She was smart but not smarter than him. He knew she could never beat him at anything. He also felt confident that if he shot some sparks her way, he could light her fire. He estimated it would take no more than three dates…and when it came time, he wouldn't have to ask her more than once. He did get the sense she was like a shy, soft-shelled crab, and if he couldn't lure her out of her shell, he would just devour her, shell and all. He might have to put in a little more effort than normal, because she didn't seem easily excitable. This he could tell by the frown on her face as she watched him eat. He made her wait while he finished his sandwich. As he ate, he thought this sexy little crustation doesn't stand a chance against me.

With the sandwich in his belly he spoke, "There has been another accident at this building. Alice Parker was found dead in the pool early this morning."

Celeste sat staring at him for a moment in shock. Oh God… poor Maybel, Celeste thought knowing Maybel and Alice had been close friends for many years. "Alice drowned?" Celeste finally asked.

"That's what we think. You were with her yesterday afternoon, weren't you?" Bahn went into detective mode, and his voice sounded stern once he'd finished his little egg sandwich.

Being an insurance claims adjuster, Celeste knew to give an accurate timeline, so she answered, "Yes, we all gathered by the pool around 4 p.m. yesterday and had some drinks and snacks. We never went swimming while I was down there. I left and came back upstairs sometime around 7 p.m."

Bahn crossed his right ankle over his left knee, his body language showing his confidence and dominance. He asked, "What kind of drinks did you have?"

"I made a pitcher of margaritas," Celeste said with her mind and heart racing. What the hell happened to Alice? I wonder if Maybel knows yet. She'll be devastated, Celeste thought.

"On a Saturday night, instead of going out with your boyfriend, you hung out with two ladies in their seventies?" Bahn asked.

Celeste assessed him too. She pegged him as a smug, insensitive asshole. She knew he wasn't smarter than her. She also picked up on the fact that he was really a nerd underneath it all, but because of his good looks, people mistakenly thought him to be cool. "Three," she said.

"What?" Bahn crumpled up his sandwich bag.

"Three. There were three ladies in their late seventies that I hung out with yesterday afternoon by the pool. Maybel, Alice and Janet," Celeste clarified.

"Oh, that's right. I've already spoken with Maybel and Janet. Your story pretty much lines up with theirs. Are there any security cameras out by the pool?" he inquired.

"I think you know there aren't," she responded. If Detective Bahn thought playing dumb was a tactic that would make her let her guard down with him, he was mistaken. Celeste was an expert in getting people to let their guards down. She also knew exactly how to use silence as a weapon.

He smiled again, a Cheshire cat smile, and looked at her for a long time. He liked her quick mind.

She took a deep breath and asked him if he had any more questions for her with him responding, "Do you know how much Alice had to drink yesterday?"

"We all had two margaritas each. That's all that was in the pitcher. Look, if you're thinking this was an accident because she had too much to drink, it couldn't have been," Celeste said in protest before he'd even said it.

"And why is that, Miss Ravenna? It is Miss, isn't it?" He ran a hand through his sandy hair.

"Because she only had two drinks, and that was spread out between 4 p.m. and 7 p.m. She was fine when I left. Plus, she was an experienced swimmer," Celeste answered.

Bahn took another look around her condo and wished he could hang out all day. It smelled of coffee and warm honey. "I've seen it happen before," he replied causally, "when someone has too much to drink. They get careless and relax too much." He dismissed her comments to elicit a reaction from her. He loved nothing more than a game of cat and mouse, especially with a mouse as pretty as Celeste.

He's trying to make me angry, she thought. She asked, "Did you find her swim cover-up?"

"Her what?"

"Her swimsuit cover-up. It was a black dress with bright flowers on it. That's what she was wearing over her bathing suit. If she went swimming, she would have taken it off," Celeste explained.

He uncrossed his legs and said, "Oh that—yes we found it. One of our officers said it was folded up in her beach bag."

"You think she was so intoxicated that she couldn't swim, but she took the time and care to fold up her swimsuit cover-up and put it in her bag?" Celeste asked defensively. She pointed to her chin feeling uncomfortable and said, "By the way you have something on your face…" She crinkled up her nose as her voice trailed off.

Detective Bahn wiped egg yolk off his chin and after a long pause, he said, "When the officers arrived, she was wearing a swim cap."

"Well see! That proves my point, Detective Bahn. If she was so drunk as to not be in the condition to be able to swim safely, she wouldn't have carefully put on her swim cap either," Celeste said and felt as if she was pleading a case in court.

"Brian. Call me Brian. Please. And I've seen people change their clothes when they're drunk," he said and smiled again.

"Brian, you're going to check the security cameras in the lobby, aren't you?" Celeste hoped this could all be figured out.

"We sure are, but as you already know, there are exits out of your building in the stairwells, and if someone goes out one of those, then there are no security cameras there to capture that. There's also a side entrance to the pool from the street, and if someone used it, they would not have to go through the lobby to get to the pool," Detective Bahn said.

Celeste got a chill again. "You'll do a toxicology report on Alice, right? That will show her blood alcohol level." Celeste wasn't sure why she felt the need to tell him what to do. Of course, they would do this, or maybe they wouldn't if they thought it was an accident.

"We will. But that, and the footage from the security cameras remains to be seen," he said. He got up and headed towards the front door. "Oh, by the way, can I get your number in case I have any other questions?"

Celeste felt her face burn as she gave him her cell phone number. He punched it into his phone and smiled again, a smile that would make the Cheshire cat's look sad. He suddenly remembered to be considerate and said, "I am very sorry for the loss of your friend, Alice. We will do everything we can to figure out what really happened to her." Then he lowered his voice, leaned in a little, locked eyes on her, and said, "Remember, keep your door locked at all times, Miss Ravenna." He saluted her and walked away.

Chapter Eight

Mansions in Heaven

Not too long after Detective Brain Bahn left, another knock landed on Celeste's door. Celeste and Maybel sat on her couch and talked. Maybel cried, and Celeste hugged her. Celeste knew this was going to be difficult for Maybel. She was patient with Maybel as she tried to process it. Celeste didn't go shopping that day. "May she rest in peace now," Celeste said.

Maybel nodded and said, "Mansions in heaven."

In the days to follow Alice Parker's death, Maybel found out Alice's daughter was going to have the funeral for Alice up near Pinewood, a small sleepy town in Northern California where Alice's daughter lived. They would do this a few weeks later, after the coroner released her body and the autopsy was done.

Since Maybel no longer drove, Celeste offered to drive her up there for the service, and they invited Janet along too. Since it was a bit of a drive, Celeste got a couple of days off. Celeste would be off the Thursday and Friday of the week of Alice's funeral and hoped that everyone at work would be able to handle their problems and claims without her. She really needed the break but going to a funeral wasn't exactly a break. She also asked Alex Graham her neighbor to water her plants for her and feed her bird Birino. Normally if she needed anything like that, she'd ask Maybel, Janet or Alice but couldn't in this scenario. The little bit of family she had lived too far away, and since Alex had asked her to collect his mail when he went out of town, she hoped he'd return the favor.

"Hi Celeste. How are you?" Alex gave her a friendly greeting when she went to his door.

Celeste wrung her hands. "I'm good. I hate to trouble you, but I was wondering if I could ask you a favor."

He smiled a big toothy smile. "Sure, what do you need?"

Celeste explained her, Maybel, and Janet were going out of town for a few days to attend Alice's funeral and hoped he could water her plants and feed her bird for her. She only had a few plants. There was one on the end of her kitchen counter that needed sun light, two on her bookshelves, and one in her office. He'd also need to put out bird seed for Birino and make sure he had fresh water. "If I put all the bird seed out when I leave, he'll eat it all of it within the first day," she said and laughed.

"That shouldn't be a problem at all. Real shame about Alice. She was a nice lady. Maybe the HOA Board should consider having a lifeguard down there at the pool, you know, so it's safe for anyone swimming by themselves," he said.

Celeste smiled politely and nodded. Her heart hurt over all of this. "That's a good idea, Alex." She gave Alex her spare key, told him exactly which days she would be gone, and thanked him again.

On Thursday morning of that week, they set out to drive up to Northern California very early. Janet sat in the front, and Maybel sat in the back. One thing they could agree on during the drive was to listen to Elvis. They all loved Elvis. It was a nice drive, and they made a few stops along the way to eat, rest, or stretch their legs. They got to Pinewood very late Thursday night and checked into the bed and breakfast Celeste found online and booked for them. The service was to be on Friday afternoon.

Celeste didn't know about the other two, but she fell asleep about a minute after her head hit the pillow. She booked a room for herself and a second room that Janet and Maybel wanted to share. It was quiet, and the drive took a lot out of her. Come morning she felt pretty good. She showered and got ready quickly as she was hungry and wanted to go downstairs to get breakfast. The day before, they agreed to meet downstairs at 8 a.m.

They ate their breakfast in the main dining room, and the coffee was good. There wasn't much Celeste could eat, as it was mostly pastries and fruit. She tried to avoid gluten, dairy and sugar. She grabbed some granola made with oats and nuts and ate that dry with her coffee. The ladies discussed the plan for the day like how long it would take to get to the church for the service and what time they should leave. They already sent flowers to the church ahead of time. Celeste brought a condolence card they all singed and put some money in for Alice's daughter Megan. They went back to their rooms to finish getting ready for the funeral.

Celeste brought a black wrap dress that tied at the waist with cap sleeves, and of course she brought her black wedge heels. Maybel wore a black suit jacket with a white blouse, black skirt, and her orthopedic shoes. Janet wore a black dress that had little white flecks on it and some black pumps. All in all, when the piled back into the car, it was obvious they were going to a funeral. None of them said much for a while on the drive to the church. The mood felt somber, and the air in the car felt heavy.

Celeste finally spoke, "Well, at least now Alice is in a better place and at peace."

"Mansions in heaven in our Father's house," Maybel said from the back seat.

"I can't wait to live in a mansion in heaven," Janet continued, "I've rented at Regal Palms for many years, and I love living there. But I often wonder what heaven will be like."

Maybel let out a deep breath and quietly said, "No mind can really imagine what heaven will be like. It is beyond our understanding, just like the galaxy."

They found the old Lutheran church in another quaint town quite easily. A collage of pictures of Alice and her family sat on an easel in the vestibule of the church along with different flower arrangements. There were several pictures of Alice from her youth, and it was obvious she loved to swim. In one picture she held a huge trophy after winning some sort of swim competition.

The three ladies introduced themselves to Alice's daughter, gave her their condolences, and took their seats for the service. During the service, two different family members got up and spoke about Alice and read some bible verses. They played three different songs which were all classic Christian hymns—Amazing Grace, I'll Fly Away and That Old Rugged Cross. It was a beautiful service for a beautiful lady, and Celeste could feel that Alice was loved. She felt the tears burn in her eyes as they sang the lyrics about laying down their trophies and exchanging them for a crown. Celeste's heart felt heavy, and her body felt like lead. The funeral was draining her.

Maybel reached over and handed Celeste a tissue. She said to her, "Alice is wearing her crown in heaven." Maybel wiped her eyes too.

Everyone exited the church when the service ended and followed the processional to the graveyard for the burial. Alice was laid to rest. Following the burial, the family invited everyone to a reception at their home. It turned out to be quite a long day, and the mood still felt somber. The gals drove over to Alice's daughter's house and made chit chat with the others at the reception. As Celeste mingled, she heard various conversations like, "such a shame this happened", "well at least she died doing the thing that she loved", and "this still doesn't make any sense she was such a good swimmer".

The family served a nice buffet with a chicken casserole they said was Alice's favorite. They also served fresh fruit and veggie trays, salads, breads, cold cuts and various desserts. Celeste was ravenous. Her handful of granolas hadn't gone very far. She didn't want to be rude, so she filled up her plate with some casserole. She also took salad, crudité and few pieces of cold cuts. She sat down in a corner of the living room by herself and dug in. Maybel and Janet were still chatting with Alice's daughter.

With her mouth full of food, Celeste heard her cell phone bing, and she knew she had a text. She hoped it wasn't from work.

She set her plate down and took out her phone. The text was from a sender that wasn't a contact in her phone, and it read: **Alice's blood alcohol level was .02%**

Celeste knew the text was from Detective Brian Bahn. She added him into her phone as one of her contacts. She sat there and took another bite of the casserole. It was delicious, a creamy chicken divan with broccoli and cheesy breadcrumbs on the top. It did seem like something Alice would have loved.

If her blood alcohol level was .02%, and the legal limit for driving is .08%, she was definitely not intoxicated while she was swimming. Alice would have been fine to swim, just as Celeste thought. She knew Alice's death was not an accidental drowning. A shiver slithered up her spine and rattled her brain. She texted Detective Bahn back: **Did you find anything on the security cameras?**

Detective Bahn texted her back: **Nothing of particular interest and nothing incriminating**

The text was a bit of a fib from Detective Bahn. Something on the security camera video did interest him quite a bit, but it wasn't relevant to the case. When he saw Celeste on the security footage walking through the lobby in her light-yellow sun dress, well, that interested him very much. She looked ethereal, and the fabric of her dress glowed in the sunlight that shined through the glass doors and windows in the lobby. The light-weight fabric of her summer dress made her look so soft. "Pause it right there," he told the technician. For several moments longer than he needed to, Bahn gazed at Celeste's image on the screen.

The technician asked if he saw something.

"No…sorry…my mistake. Continue on," he instructed.

Celeste Ravenna's image haunted Detective Brian Bahn of the Sunshine Beach Police. Murderers, rapists and drug dealers he could make leave his mind easily at the end of the day, but not Celeste. She stayed for a while.

Chapter Nine

The Ice Is Starting to Melt

On the drive back home after Alice's funeral, they took two days instead of one. They stopped off at another little town called Santa Vienna and stayed the night there but not before doing some shopping. Celeste purchased an antique brass bird cage she knew her little birdie Birino would love. While she always left the door to his bird cage open, so he could go in and out as he pleased, Birino knew the newspaper in the cage was where to "do his business". Her colorful little finch would love his new home.

They got back late Sunday afternoon, and Celeste felt exhausted again from the daunting drive. She looked forward to going back to work to take her mind off things. Her work week of deadlines, demands, questions, claims, adjusted claims, claims rejections, issues for her to resolve and meetings made it zoom by. She sailed through it all and didn't think about Jennifer or Alice.

Thursday night for dinner Maybel cooked a pot roast, yams and green beans. Maybel made the best pot roast. She threw pepperoncinis in the crock pot that gave it a distinct flavor along with a stick of butter and a packet of gravy and Ranch seasoning. While they sat at Maybel's Formica table, she pulled apart the pot roast with her fork and said, "I think Vick killed Alice."

While Vick wasn't her favorite person, he hardly seemed a killer. Celeste asked why Maybel thought this.

"He always hated that Alice would swim in the pool after curfew," she said with certainty.

"But that is hardly a reason to kill someone," Celeste protested.

"Well, Alice was so insistent that they fix the cracks in the pool, and that drove Vick crazy. You know, he likes to be in control. He wanted to spend the money in the special assessment fund elsewhere. Lots of people have been bugging him and the board about the limited parking, the faulty electrical in the laundry room, and not enough washers and dryers. Plus, you know he always had a thing for Jennifer—following her around like a puppy dog," Maybel said.

Celeste looked at Maybel and thought she'd lost her mind. Grief does strange things to people. Celeste knew Maybel wasn't just grieving the loss of her friend Alice but the loss of her husband George as well. A new loss always reminds you of an old loss. "You think Vick Arnold, President of Regal Palms Homeowners Association, killed Jennifer Riley and Alice Parker?"

Maybel nodded her head emphatically. "YES!"

Celeste took a deep breath, let it out, and then very gently said, "Maybel, while all of those things are true, I just don't think Vick Arnold killed both of those women." She knew Maybel never liked Vick so it would be easy to think something negative of him, but this was a little too much. Yes, Vick rudely snapped like a turtle, and was a stickler for the rules, but that hardly made him a killer, Celeste rationalized. "Let's play some cards," she said to Maybel to get Maybel's mind off the deaths. After about three rounds of Go Fish, (Celeste refused to play poker with Maybel because she got too competitive) she said goodnight and headed back to her place…but not before having some of Maybel's homemade macaroons for dessert.

The next day after work, she was on her way up to her place when she heard a male voice shout, "Hold the elevator!" She turned and saw her neighbor Alex running towards it.

"Alex, funny meeting you here," she tried to joke. He didn't laugh, and he seemed to be in a bad mood. He was out of breath and looked a little sweaty. "It's really hot out today," Celeste tried to make conversation as they rode up to the ninth floor together.

"Tell me about it, and that parking structure across the street is like an oven. Plus, my car got nicked the other day, and I don't know who hit it," he said.

"Oh, I'm sorry to hear that," Celeste said sympathetically.

Alex reached into his pocket. "By the way, here's your key back," he said.

"Thank you again for helping," Celeste said and meant it.

"I never actually saw Birino. I don't know if he was hiding from me, or if he's just shy," Alex said and chuckled. "But I still changed his water and made sure he had bird seed."

"Yeah, he can be kind of elusive at times," Celeste said and smiled. The bell dinged to indicate they reached their floor.

Birino perched himself on the top shelf of her bookcase in his favorite spot. She smiled. It was Friday, and the whole weekend stood ahead of her. She made herself a quick dinner by heating up some frozen meatballs, putting marinara sauce on them, and pouring herself a big glass of wine. She sat down on her couch to eat and stared out her windows. The sun started its descent. A soft glow around the city illuminated the buildings. As she ate, she thought about what Maybel said about Vick, and it nagged at her. She decided to reach out to Detective Bahn. After dinner, she sent him a text that read: **Was Vick Arnold (President of the HOA) on the security cameras on the Saturday night of Alice's drowning?**

Two minutes later he texted back: **Why would you like to know?**

Celeste let out half of a laugh and texted back: **Maybel thinks he killed Alice Parker and Jennifer Riley.**

A minute later, Celeste's phone rang. Startled, she contemplated not answering Detective Bahn's call. No, you have to answer because you were just texting with him, she thought. "Hello," she greeted softly.

The cliché deep, husky voice greeted her back. "Good evening, Miss Ravenna."

Celeste felt awkward and spoke quickly, "Maybel has this crazy theory that Vick Arnold killed Alice Parker and Jennifer Riley," Celeste explained Maybel's reasoning to him and waited through a pause.

"Well, I can tell you that the only time on the security camera Vick appeared in the lobby was around 7 p.m. on Saturday. Then a few minutes later he came back through the lobby and went up the elevator." Celeste knew this was the time Vick came out and reminded them all of the 9 p.m. curfew and explained that to Detective Bahn...but she also knew Vick could have gone down the stairwell, out an exit that leads straight outside, and gone through the pool gate entrance off the street.

"Anyone else on the cameras in the lobby were going in and out of the main entrance. The only other ones going through the side entrance to the pool were Vick, you, Maybel, Janet, Alice and a family with a couple of little kids. Nice hat by the way."

Celeste felt embarrassed when she realized he saw her in the silly hat she wore briefly with her summer dress.

"Then, early the next morning a gal who works for the property management company with bright red hair and very short bangs," he rubbed his index finger across his forehead as he remembered, "arrived at work. She went out the side entrance to the pool to do the daily visual inspection. That's when she found Alice and called the police."

Well, this doesn't help at all, she thought. After another long silence between them, Bahn spoke. "There was something interesting with Jennifer Riley's autopsy report." Bahn paused again and his game of cat and mouse drove Celeste crazy. He figured out how to press her buttons and enjoyed the reaction he could elicit from her.

She let out a frustrated sigh and finally asked, "What was that?"

"There were strangulation marks around her neck. No prints because the killer used gloves. Jennifer was dead before she hit the ground," Bahn said. Celeste felt a sick feeling of panic racing through her. *No wonder he told me to lock my door,* she thought.

Radio silence on the phone again.

"Miss Ravenna?"

Celeste took a deep breath. "You can call me Celeste," she said.

"Celeste, I need for you to be very careful. I do believe there is a murderer loose in your building."

No shit, Celeste thought. "Do you have any idea who?" She hoped he'd have some sort of lead.

"At this time, we don't have any real suspects. We've been going through Jennifer's emails and phone records. She had a lot of male admirers," Bahn said.

"Was Vick Arnold one of them?"

"Yes. There are some emails between him and her. They are mostly her complaining about a plumbing problem with her shower she believed should have been covered under the HOA. Vick told her it wasn't covered under the HOA, and it was her responsibility to take care of it...but then he offered to personally help her out with it," Bahn said.

Celeste asked, "What does that mean?"

"I really shouldn't say. I'm not at liberty to go into any great detail about a pending case, but since I trust you, and I'm concerned for your safety, I will tell you…but you have to promise not to tell anyone else, especially Maybel. I get the sense that if Maybel knows something, then the whole building would know," Bahn said.

Celeste smiled to herself. Bahn was correct in thinking that. He dangled a piece of information out in front of her again but was taking his sweet time in letting her know what it was. "Ok, I promise."

Bahn went on to explain, "The emails are a little vague, but from what I can gather, he offers to take care of the plumbing problem for her in some sort of services exchange."

Celeste wondered, "You mean…like sex?"

"Yes, a plumbing / sex exchange…but I think Vick was the one who really got his pipes cleaned out," Bahn joked.

Celeste laughed and then instantly felt guilty for laughing.

Bahn smiled on his end of the phone. That was the first time he made her laugh. He was fascinated by Celeste. Most women threw themselves at Bahn, especially if they found out he was a cop, or if they saw him in uniform in his younger days, but Celeste didn't seem interested. She was cold to him. Maybe he could melt some of those layers of ice off her. He got serious again. "There is more," he went on. "It seemed Jennifer did that a lot…traded sex for something she wanted. We've been checking alibis of the men that she'd been in contact with recently, but so far everyone has one…except for Vick."

"Maybel said that Jennifer told her mother the night before she died, she just got engaged." Celeste hoped Bahn would have some insight into that.

"Yes, she told us that as well, but nothing in her phone or email records indicated that. She was also not wearing an engagement ring when she died," Bahn said.

Celeste asked, "Did you find one in her condo?"

"No. By the way, what do you know about Billy Cheng?"

"The rich guy that lives in the penthouse? Not much. He has a pretty wife named Lily that looks a lot like Jennifer did. Maybel said there was a rumor going around that Billy and Jennifer were having an affair, but I have no way of knowing that for sure," Celeste answered.

"It's not a rumor," Bahn stated with authority.

"What?"

"Her phone records show she was texting with Billy a lot in her final days. By the content of the texts, it is pretty obvious they had been intimate. There was a night his wife wasn't home, and he invited her up to the penthouse. Jennifer had sent him some topless photos of herself sunbathing on the roof too." Celeste asked if Billy had an alibi for the morning Jennifer died. "His wife Lily said he was with her...but I've seen spouses lie for each other before."

"I would think that if Jennifer had been up on the roof sunbathing topless, Billy would have seen her," Celeste said.

"Lily could have seen her too," Bahn added.

"This is puzzling to me. I mean, let's say Billy and/or Lily did have something to do with Jennifer's demise, what would they have against Alice? What would be the common thread between Jennifer and Alice?"

"Nothing that I've been able to come up with, and believe me, we've been digging around as much as we can." Bahn let out a heavy sign.

"This is so disturbing. Will you please keep me posted if you find out anything else?"

Bahn said, "I sure will. Have a good night, Celeste."

"You too, Brian." Celeste hit the end call button and sat on her couch for a while. The city lights were bright against the dark back drop of the night. She wondered what the heck was really going on in the building.

After her call with Bahn, Celeste also began to wonder if Maybel was right about Vick being the killer. He was wound pretty tight, and he did have a bit of a temper. Maybe he snapped. But two murders? It still seemed wild. Maybe Alice and Jennifer's deaths were done by two different people. There was no way Celeste was going to figure it out that night, nor was it her job to she thought to herself.

To help her sleep, she watched a black and white movie from the old movie channel. Celeste was partial to the Noir film genre because back then they really knew how to do glamour. The fancy coats, long gloves, diamond necklaces, fedora hats, pin striped suits, pencil skirts, pearl broaches, pin curled hair, and beautiful cars all enthralled her. There seemed to always be a nightclub scene with show girls, sequined gowns, tuxedos and cocktails. Celeste munched on some popcorn while she watched the movie and waited to find out who the killer was. She thought about how life imitated art sometimes. Would she ever know who the killer in their building was?

Chapter Ten

Mums the Word

The next day for Saturday lunch, Celeste served Maybel turkey and salami sandwiches on toasted English muffins with mayonnaise, mustard, sun dried tomatoes and spinach leafs instead of lettuce. Maybel said she never thought to use spinach instead of lettuce on a sandwich, and she really liked it. They drank coffee and ate chocolate mousse made from coconut milk for dessert. Celeste felt a little guilty for not telling Maybel about her call with Detective Bahn, but she had been sworn to secrecy.

"Janet says they'll be starting on the electrical this week in the laundry room," Maybel said and scraped the bottom of her mousse cup to get it all.

"I think that if you or Janet need to do laundry, you two should go to the laundry room together. Use the buddy system."

Maybel took a sip of her coffee and contemplated this. "I guess that couldn't hurt."

After Maybel left, Celeste got caught up on some housework including cleaning Birino's new cage. She also paid some bills online. She owed her HOA dues for the month. She did it old school and took a check downstairs. There was an onsite property management office in the lobby, and a staff member was there seven days a week. The lobby chairs were new, but they were a mid-century style. A good choice in her opinion. The lobby had phone booths back in the day. Now the phones were gone, and they hung artwork in those slots.

She walked to the property management office and stopped by the bulletin board. She liked to look at it in case there were any important notices. That day she saw a reminder about the pool hours. Geez Vick is really stuck on that, she thought. There was an ad saying someone on the second floor needed a babysitter and an ad for a dog walker offering their services. She wondered if they could help Birino exercise. She also noticed the waiting list for reserved parking listed eighteen people on it.

Janice sat at the property management desk that day, and Celeste liked Janice. She'd known her for a while, and she had a good sense of humor. She rented one of the condo units at Regal Palms, had a happy face and very short bangs. "Hi there!" she greeted.

"Your hair cut is so cute! How have you been?" Celeste asked noticing Janice's bangs were way above her drawn on eyebrows.

"Oh, you know—the usual 'my toilet isn't flushing', 'there is a light out in the hallway', 'my neighbor's dog won't shut up', 'the trash shoot is full', 'the dryer ate up my quarters'…all in a day's work," she replied.

Celeste leaned her elbows on the counter and handed Janice her check. "I don't envy you," she said trying to sound understanding.

"Horrible business about that gal Jennifer and dear Alice. I've worked here ten years and rented here for five and never seen anything like this! The gossip is they suspect foul play." Janice scratched her head with her pen.

Celeste looked away not wanting to say anything.

Janice asked, "Do you really think Jennifer killed herself?"

Celeste looked Janice in the eye and said, "No."

"You wouldn't believe what I saw Jennifer doing in the lobby one time. She was back in the corner with some guy tucked away in one of the old phone booths, and I think they thought they were out of view…but I could see her head bobbing up and down. Just between you and me, I think she was a prostitute," Janice whispered even though Celeste and she were the only ones in the office.

"That's what I've heard, but I really have no way of knowing for sure," Celeste said.

Janice leaned in and whispered, "You know, I'm the one that found Alice. I'm still having nightmares about it." Janice closed her eyes and put her hand over her heart to calm herself.

Celeste's face looked pained, "I'll bet." She sympathized and shook her head. "Did you notice anything suspicious when you found Alice?" Celeste hoped for something.

"No, not really. That's the same question that hot cop asked me too," Janice said. "Alice did have on her swim cap on though, I remember that…and the second gate to the pool, the one that is off the street, that was unlocked. Really, I shouldn't even tell you that. The property management company doesn't want any of us staff talking about it. They're afraid people will get freaked out and move out of the building. That would be bad for business, so Vick said we're not allowed to talk about it."

Celeste reassured her, "Mums the word." She thought to herself, if the outside gate to the pool was unlocked, then that was obviously how the killer got to the pool without going through the lobby. They chatted a bit longer about Alice's funeral, and then Celeste said goodbye.

Around dinner time, she didn't feel like cooking, so she ordered a Cobb salad from a local restaurant and had it delivered. She watched another old black and white movie while she ate. The amplified drama of the Noir film genre, and the use of shadows to help tell the story made it very intense. The killer lurked in the distance. This you knew because his silhouette appeared on the wall behind the victim.

The movie ended and after some restlessness, she stood by her bedroom window and stared at the full moon. She wanted to know the truth about what happened to Jennifer and Alice but feared she never would. Who was Jennifer's fiancée?

The next morning, she slept in late. She didn't mean to, but the tossing and turning kept her up in the night. She decided to make a relaxing day for herself by reading and watching more movies. She threw the ingredients for chili into her crockpot and gave herself a manicure and a pedicure. Later, she lounged around, ate a bowl of chili and enjoyed another movie from the Noir film genre. A shootout between the bad guys and the cops took place. They were on the run through the streets of New York. Later, a jilted lover took revenge and did the old double cross.

The R&R over the weekend helped Celeste sail into her work week.

Mark

Mark Summons liked his routine, and he liked things organized. Every Thursday he did his laundry in the Regal Palms laundry room. He even left work early at 2 p.m. on Thursdays just so he could get a jump on traffic and get into the laundry room before anyone else did. The laundry room housed three washers and three dryers. This was perfect for Mark as every Thursday he did three loads of laundry. He separated them into three categories: his clothes, his bedding and his bathroom towels. He didn't like that other people used the washers and dryers as well. Being a bit of neat freak, he liked to do what some called a "pre-wash cleansing cycle". He put laundry detergent in all three washers and ran them without anything in them first. This washed away any dirt or germs left behind from a previous resident. Essentially Mark did six loads of laundry every Thursday.

That Thursday while completely occupying the laundry room, he shooed away at least four different people who thought they could come in and do their laundry while he was there. Fat chance, he thought. Mark was very territorial and wasn't about to change his routine. After six loads in the washers, he switched his clothes to the dryers. He put quarters in the first two dryers, and they started fine. The laundry room felt warm and smelled of detergent. The hum of the dryers calmed him. Mark always liked that. He added his wet bedding to the third dryer and put the quarters in the slot. That time, the dryer didn't start.

He shook and kicked the dryer and tried to start it again. Nothing. He pulled the dryer out from the wall a bit and looked behind it. The cord looked a little loose. He crouched down and reached back behind the dryer to plug it in all the way…but that frayed cord waited for him like a snake ready to bite. When it did, he felt a sharp immobilizing pain in his arm and couldn't let go of the cord. In a flash, the electricity barreled through his body like a lightning bolt and burst out his foot. Lights went out for Mark Summons. That was the last time he used his fabric softener.

Chapter Eleven

A Bird in the Hand

Thursday morning Celeste's alarm buzzed her at 4:30 a.m. like an annoying little fly that wouldn't go away. She popped one coffee pod, two coffee pods, three coffee pods…this enabled her to get ready quickly. She chose an outfit of a deep burgundy wine-colored blouse with a sweetheart neckline and little silver shiny buttons up the front. She paired it with her standard black straight skirt and black wedge heels. Dark burgundy lipstick punched her lips hard with color and winged cat eyeliner outlined her dark gypsy eyes. She topped it all off with a diamond rhinestone barrette on the right side of her long dark hair.

She left the parking structure around 5:30 a.m. and got to work by 6 a.m. She found going in early gave her a fighting chance at getting caught up and gave her a jump on the day. Early hours gifted her at least two hours of "quiet time" to work on things before the staff started to filter in and the phones went live.

Late in the day, she noticed a missed call on her cell phone from Maybel. She didn't have time to call her back before heading into her last meeting of the day. She could talk to Maybel at dinner later. She escaped work at 5 o'clock. Emails were still flying in, but those problems could wait until the next day. The music on the radio kept her form getting annoyed at the traffic on her way home.

She took the elevator up and felt relieved it was empty. After a long day, she wasn't in the mood to make idle chit chat. She walked down the hall, and when she turned the corner, saw Detective Brian Bahn leaning against the wall by her front door. His thumbs were hooked into his pants pockets. It startled her to see him there, and she stopped dead in her wedge heeled tracks. The Macho stance, she thought.

He wore his outdated blazer again. "Hello Celeste."

"Hi Brian, what brings you here?" When she unlocked her door, he noticed she smelled like lavender and coconut. He followed her in and closed the door behind them. She set her purse down on one of her violet barstools. She turned to face him, and Birino flew from the bookcase and landed on Bahn's right shoulder. Birino eagerly greeted Bahn. Celeste said surprised, "He likes you."

Bahn put his left hand up to his shoulder and Birino walked onto it. Bahn gently scratched his little head. "What kind of bird is he?" Bahn wondered.

"He's a finch, and he's a little bit overweight. He loves his bird seed." After a few seconds of bonding between Birino and Bahn, Celeste's little birdie flew back up to his perch on the top shelf of her bookcase. Bahn walked over to the bookcase and looked around a bit. Celeste wondered what brought him to her place.

"You have quite a collection of books here...do you have that one that talks about men and women being from different planets? I bet you have a book on astrology, and you think you can figure someone out based on their sign," he said and laughed. He continued to poke around while Celeste stood with one hand on her hip and the other on a barstool waiting for him to get to the point. He asked, "Is this a bull?"

"Yes, those are book ends—one is a bear and the other a bull. You know, for the stock market," she answered.

"Ah yes, these are so cool." Bahn picked up the bull. "Geez this is heavy!"

Celeste watched him fondle the bull and explained it was made of bronze which gave it the weight.

"Do you read a lot in your spare time? Do you do anything more exciting than reading?" He grinned at her. His teasing fell flat with Celeste.

"The best way to let the mind travel is to read. A good book can transport you through a literary time machine. What brings you here Detective Bahn?"

Bahn set the bull back down and finally turned around to look at her. He eyed the buttons on her shirt, and asked, "Did you know Mark Summons?"

Celeste frowned and thought for a few seconds. "I don't think so. That name doesn't ring a bell. Does he live in the building?"

"He did," Bahn said only giving one little piece of information.

"Did something happen to him?"

Bahn moved a little closer to her, lowered his voice, and said, "He was found dead this afternoon around 3:45 p.m. in the laundry room of the building."

Celeste felt startled and stepped back from Bahn. She asked, "What happened to him?"

"It appears he was electrocuted. It looked like the cord for one of the dryers was frayed. He probably tried to plug it in," Bahn explained.

"So, it was an accident?" Celeste's stomach felt sick again.

"Probably. We dusted for fingerprints, but in a situation like this, there will be dozens of them everywhere," Bahn said.

That made sense to Celeste. She knew most tenants used the laundry room. "This is three deaths in the building in the last two months," she said counting.

Bahn nodded.

Celeste struggled to believe it. "Well, I don't mean to be rude, but if you don't have any more questions for me, I need to get going. Maybel is expecting me for dinner tonight."

Bahn smiled the Cheshire cat smile again. "She invited me too. I'll walk over there with you."

Celeste let out a breath and said, "How nice of her. Shall we get going then?" Celeste led the way and could feel his eyes on her back side.

"Come in. Come in you two! Dinner is just about ready. Detective Bahn, I hope you like meatloaf," Maybel said giving them a warm greeting.

"Oh, I love it. Thank you again for inviting me. Since my divorce, I don't get a home cooked meal very often," he said.

He's divorced, what a surprise Celeste thought sarcastically. "Maybel makes the best meatloaf I've ever had," Celeste said.

Maybel smiled. "The secret is to sauté the onions and peppers before mixing up all the ingredients."

Celeste walked over to the kitchen table and noticed three place settings. Even though it was a square table with four sides to it, Maybel put one place setting on one side and two place settings very close together on the opposite side. Maybel noticed Celeste looking at the table and hurried over. "This is my spot right here. I put my cholesterol medication right next to it. Celeste, you and Detective Bahn can sit on the other side."

"It's Brian. Please call me Brian," he said, and smiled at Maybel.

Maybel grinned from ear to ear too.

Apparently, it's a smile fest tonight, Celeste thought. She walked around to the other side of the table and sat down. Brian sat next to her so close their legs were touching. Celeste felt a spark from the connection and quickly moved her leg away from the heat. Maybel carried over the food to the table—meatloaf, mashed potatoes, and roasted glazed carrots. Crescent rolls and salad were already on the table. Maybel made conversation with Detective Bahn and got some information out of him. He was from back east somewhere like Boston, in his mid-forties, divorced twice, no kids, hobbies were shooting guns and watching Game of Thrones. None of the information surprised Celeste. Maybe you should ask him what his favorite color is, she thought. Maybel went on with her twenty questions, and to Celeste's amusement, Maybel did eventually ask Detective Bahn his favorite color. When he responded 'burgundy', she smiled and looked at Celeste's blouse.

Celeste inquired, "How long have you been a detective?"

"Let's see, I made detective about ten years ago," he answered.

"I bet you've caught a lot of bad guys," Maybel mused.

He winked at her and said, "A few."

Maybel blushed.

Celeste tried to keep an eye roll at bay and changed the subject again. "Maybel, did you know Mark Summons?"

Maybel put down her fork. "I didn't know him very well. He kept to himself mostly. I think he was some sort of engineer. He lived on the third floor next to Jennifer Riley. He's only lived here about three years. He had a regular schedule in the laundry room and never let anyone move in on it."

"Maybel has been very helpful to us in the investigations. She provided us with a lot of information." Bahn praised her, but Celeste wasn't sure if he was serious or not.

Maybel smiled proudly and said, "Well, you know, I am one of the original residents here. My late husband George and I moved here in 1958."

"Who found Mark in the laundry room?" Celeste asked.

"Vick Arnold! That little jerk!" Maybel answered before Detective Bahn could. "When are you going to arrest him? He's behind all this. I know it. I feel it in my bones," Maybel said with certainty.

"We don't have any hard evidence against him," Bahn said and ate more meatloaf.

Maybel baked an apple crumble for dessert with oats on the topping. Celeste stuck around a little longer. How could she say no to dessert? Detective Bahn complemented Maybel on her cooking a few more times, as she fawned over him serving him coffee. Celeste felt tired and wanted to go to sleep. The crumble put her over the top. She offered to help Maybel with the dishes, but Maybel insisted that wasn't necessary. Celeste made the excuse of needing to get up early the next morning and excused herself. Bahn stood up quickly and said he'd walk her to her door.

What a gentleman, Maybel thought.

As Celeste unlocked her door, he put his hand on her shoulder. This caused Celeste to turn around and look at him. "Promise me you will be careful. There is a killer in your building. I didn't mention this at dinner, but one of the investigators said the wires didn't look like they naturally frayed. They looked like they were deliberately tampered with. We spoke with the electrician who is working on the upgrade, and he said he never touched the cord to that dryer."

Celeste didn't know what she could do. She felt helpless. Yes, she could keep her door locked. Yes, she could not go to the pool, laundry room or roof by herself. Yes, she could not trust anyone like she normally did, but if a killer came after her, what could she really do? "I will be careful. I promise."

He locked eyes with her again. "If you need anything, call me."

"I will," she said. She stepped inside, said goodnight, and closed the door.

Celeste changed into her pajamas and went into the bathroom to wash her make-up off. She heard her phone ring.

"Dear, I don't know why you are so cold to Detective Bahn. He really likes you," Maybel said.

"He's arrogant, and he acts like he thinks I'm going to sleep with him, and I haven't even decided," Celeste said.

Maybel being worldly and realistic asked, "Dear, are you going to tell me…that there is no chance…whatsoever…that you won't at some point in time in the future…end up flat on your back with him?"

"Goodnight, Maybel." Celeste hung up.

Chapter Twelve

The Halloween Party

In the weeks to follow Mark's death, things at Regal Palms were quiet. Detective Bahn searched under every rock he could. The victims' places were searched with a fine-tooth comb, dozens of fingerprints taken, phone records scoured, numerous tenants questioned, security increased, but none of this turned up anything useful.

In the September HOA board meeting, old business and new business was discussed. Most tenants were still under the impression the three recent deaths were all accidents, or a suicide. A concerned tenant raised their hand and asked about the annual Halloween mixer. "Will we be having it this year considering what happened to the gal that jumped off the roof?"

The Halloween mixer was a huge party thrown annually for all the residents at Regal Palms and held on the rooftop observation deck. After some discussion, Maybel raised her hand and stood up. She spoke with conviction, "Jennifer always loved the Halloween mixer. I think we should continue to have it in her honor…and in honor of Alice and Mark…God rest their souls." Muffled voices sprinkled through the crowd, but everyone seemed to like the idea. The board agreed and green lighted the annual Halloween mixer.

September rolled into October, and even though autumn arrived, an Indian summer still blazed red hot in Sunshine Beach. Maybel headed up the committee to organize the Halloween mixer. She tried to get Celeste involved, but Celeste refused. "I have too much going on at work to take on any extra responsibility," she said as her reason. Celeste did agree to bring food to the party, wear a costume, and invite her best friend Veronica.

Maybel kept her costume a secret, and so did Janet. Celeste on the other hand, employed Maybel's help with her costume because it required a little sewing. Celeste decided to use an old white chiffon dress with an empire waist and turn it into a toga style dress. She'd pair it with gold sandals, a gold belt, and a gold leaf crown to be some type of Greek peasant girl. She let Maybel know her plans, and Maybel happily tailored the dress to make it a perfect costume for the daughter she never had.

The party was on the weekend before Halloween. Maybel and the rest of the committee kept busy planning the food, decorations, games, prizes, and music. Billy Cheng donated $1,000 towards the party's festivities. Normally the budget was only $500, so this year the committee could go all out. They hired a D.J. and were going to have a special dance floor that lit up. They also reused the old, stored decorations from past mixers to save money.

When the Saturday night of the party arrived, Celeste took special care to do her hair and make-up. She wore her hair down in long loose waves. For her make-up, she did a dramatic smoky eye and a light-colored lip gloss that wouldn't compete with her eye make-up. The dress Maybel altered came out great. The silky chiffon type of fabric moved nicely. It originally had straps, but Maybel removed one to make it a one shouldered dress. Maybel also shortened the dress so that it hit her right above the knee. Celeste gave herself a pedicure making her toes look perfect when she put on her gold gladiator sandals. She slipped on a gold arm cuff, and then carefully put on the chaplet she found online. She looked in the mirror and wondered why couldn't she wear this lovely crown every day?

A knock at the door indicated Veronica landed at Regal Palms. Celeste opened the door to see her friend standing on the other side. Veronica Owens, an all-American beauty, dressed as an alligator in a green onesie type of pajama outfit. Her head poked out of the hood of the costume which was designed to be the alligator's mouth. Celeste tried unsuccessfully not to giggle. "Ronnie, you look fantastic. I love it!"

Veronica said, "Thank you. I was feeling a bit bloated, and I know it can get cold up on the roof, so I dressed accordingly. It was a toss-up between this or a giant hot dog costume." Veronica and Celeste worked together at an insurance company years earlier. They instantly hit it off and managed to stay close over the years, even though their careers took them on different paths. Veronica was as sharp as Celeste but not nearly as jaded about love.

"Good choice! Do you want a pre-drink?"

Veronica asked, "You mean like we get drunk before we go up to the roof?"

"Yes…but I warn you now, I get really philosophical when I drink," Celeste said.

"I get really athletic when I drink! I just want to go bowling!" Veronica swung her arm around in the same motion as to throw a strike. Then she carefully sat down on a purple barstool pulling her tail to the side to keep from sitting on it.

Celeste went into the kitchen and made some Moscow mules pouring vodka over iced ginger soda. She squeezed lime and smelt the fresh, citrusy scent. They toasted to a fun night and got caught up on their chit chat before they left. Veronica told Celeste the gory details of her most recent break up while they sipped their cocktails. "He kept wanting me to dress up as a Catholic school girl," Veronica explained.

"That's what he was into?" Celeste asked.

"That's *all* he was into," Veronica replied.

Celeste shook her head. "Oh my…"

Earlier Celeste prepared a tray of tortilla roll up sandwiches and bought a couple of bags of chips. Veronica brought a cookie tray and some bags of candy. They gathered all their food and headed up to the roof around 8:30 p.m. The party started at 7 p.m., but no one showed up on time, except for the committee and the families with children. They got off the elevator on the twelfth floor, and before even going into the stairwell they could hear and feel the music thumping. "Oh man, I forgot they got a D.J. this year," Celeste said and looked back at Veronica.

Veronica demonstrated how alligators dance the cabbage patch. "I'm ready to boogie."

The elevator dinged, and Alex Graham stepped out dressed as Batman. "Here, let me get the door for you Celeste, since your hands are full," he said and rushed past her to open the door for them.

When Celeste stepped onto the roof, her jaw dropped. The place looked great. Twinkle lights shined like stars all over the party, and the city lights created a perfect back drop for the night. The Saturday Night Fever type dance floor lit up in the middle of the rooftop with clusters of pumpkins scattered about. A papier-mache skeleton Maybel crafted years earlier hung from the roof that covered the firepit area. Music blasted from the speakers. The lyrics about attending a dead man's party didn't seem the best choice for the night considering all that took place in the last couple of months, but Celeste shrugged it off and thought when in Rome…

Children were allowed to attend the mixer but normally went home by 10 p.m. For this reason, they kept the decorations PG and not too scary. Tables set up for food were along the east side of the roof. Celeste and Veronica made their way over to them and set out the things they brought. The tables were packed full of all kinds of goodies. Celeste set down her sandwich tray between two bubbling crock pots of chili and nacho cheese. She put the chips next to a huge tray of chicken wings and a big bowl of what looked to be onion dip or hummus. She wasn't sure. Veronica put her cookies and candy down by the gooey brownies and caramel dipped apples. Tom Fitzpatrick manned the grill barbequing hot dogs and hamburgers. Another tenant toasted marshmallows at the fire pit to top off the chocolatey s'mores.

"Let's go get a burger," Celeste said to Veronica. As they made their way through the crowd over to the grill, a feather on someone's costume poked Celeste in the face. She giggled and knew it would be a fun night. "Hi Tom. This is my friend Veronica."

Tom flipped a burger, set the spatula down, and stuck out his hand to Veronica to shake it. "Well, if you ain't a gator, you gator bait," he said in reference to Veronica's costume. They chatted for a bit and Celeste felt pretty sure she saw some sparks fly between Tom and Veronica. Tom dressed as a lumber jack which suited him, Celeste thought. He grew a scruffy beard and dawned on a classic red and black checkered flannel shirt tucked into his jeans. Suspenders held it all together. He wore work boots and tucked a tiny fake plastic ax in his back pocket. Based on how Veronica giggled at him, Celeste suspected someone would be yelling "Timber!" before the night ended.

Maybel came up to them bouncing around a little. Her costume of aerobics instructor from the 1980's was complete with hot pink leg warmers and sweat bands around her wrists and head. She wore a pink and yellow striped leotard with pink tights. She looked fabulous and shouted, "Let's get physical!" Celeste suspected Maybel also pre-drank. "You ladies look great!"

"Maybel, you guys really outdid yourselves this year," Veronica gushed. Having been to a couple of parties in the past, she knew they weren't usually this elaborate.

"Yeah, we had a bigger budget this year," Maybel said. "Now Ladies, remember to drink responsibly tonight. The key is moderation, so…let's get lit!" Maybel laughed at herself and then suddenly sniffed the air and asked, "Do you smell that? Someone is smoking it. Ladies, if you'll excuse me." Maybel rushed off.

With burgers in hand, Veronica and Celeste made their way to the margarita slushy machine the committee set up, and the gals filled their cups up with the icy green sludge. "If I'm going to dance, I'm going to need more booze," Celeste said as she finished her first margarita. She shook off the brain freeze and went back in for a second one with Veronica right behind her.

Later Maybel's beloved son Jeffrey shouted Celeste's name over the music. She turned and smiled. "Jeffrey, so glad you could make it," Celeste said and reached out and hugged him. She'd met him a few times before and found him to be a very nice guy. He dressed as a monk, and next to him was a pretty woman dressed as a nun.

"This is my girlfriend Jill," he introduced the nun. Jeffrey seemed smitten with her.

"So nice to meet you. Great costumes," Celeste said admiring their couple's costume.

"Thanks. Have you seen what my mom is dressed up as? I heard her singing that old 80's song 'let me hear your body talk'," Jeffrey's said, and his face looked pained.

"Physical," Celeste said.

"What?" Jeff asked.

"The name of the song. I think she's already had a little to drink," Celeste shouted over the music.

"I think she's had a lot to drink, and I think I need a few drinks to catch up," Jeffrey replied. "Even when she's sober, she relentlessly talks to me about how she needs grandkids, so I can't even imagine what she'll say tonight."

Jeffrey's date, Jill, hooked her arm through his, winked and said, "Well I don't know how that's going to happen since we've both taken a vow of celibacy."

Celeste noticed Jeffrey blushed. She smiled at how sweet he was and waved her hand toward the margarita machine. "Feel free to help yourselves. I hope you two have a great time tonight. It also looks like someone just tapped the keg," she said and pointed to a resident who hooked the party up.

"Thanks. It's good to see you again, Celeste." Jeff and his nun moved towards the booze.

The party got louder, and folks moved out to the dance floor. Batman danced with a cheerleader. Superman Daddy twirled around with his little Superman son. A silly doctor did the twist with a spooky witch. When the D.J. played a song by the king about a burning part of his love, Veronica grabbed Celeste's hand and yanked her out on the dance floor. They spun around and bumped their hips together. Maybel and Janet quickly joined them. Janet dressed up in 1980's aerobics gear too, and her and Maybel did jumping jacks to the beat. They all shook their tail feathers to the music having a grand old time.

During the 'Monster Mash', Detective Bahn arrived and stood at the edge of the dance floor observing the party. As he scanned the crowd, he knew the killer was there somewhere. He could feel it. Evidence didn't lead him to believe that; instinct did. Then he spotted Celeste. He gazed at her and smiled to himself. He wore a costume he thought would be funny that Vick talked him into, but upon seeing Celeste, he felt nervous about it. He wanted to dance with her and searched for the nerve.

After a few songs, Celeste got tired of dancing and told Veronica she wanted to take a break. Veronica tugged on the thick green fleece of her costume that felt like an incubator at that point and said, "Ok, I'm sweating my balls off in this costume, so I can sit down for a bit and cool off."

"I'll go get us some water," Celeste said as she walked away.

Veronica called after her, "With vodka in it."

Celeste dug around in a cooler full of ice and found two bottles of water before her hand froze. She turned, and right behind her stood Detective Bahn. He nervously blurted out, "Celeste! What are you doing here? How did you dance so sexy?"

She laughed and answered, "I live here. What are you doing here?" She took note of his costume. He stood in front of her with half an avocado costume encompassing his tall body, and his head poked out of it. The outfit was complete with green tights, and a big brown seed popped out of the middle of the avocado right around where his belly was. Green paint covered his face, and green gloves adorned his hands.

"Oh…well…Maybel and Vick both invited me. They thought it would be good to have a police presence here considering everything that went on in the building over the summer. Vick kind of befriended me. I think he always wanted to be a cop," Bahn said and with a green gloved finger, he pulled on the tight face hole of his costume.

She teased him and asked, "Where are you hiding your gun?"

"Technically I'm off duty," he said.

Celeste knew enough cops to know even when they are off duty, they still carry…somewhere. She decided not to push it. "What made you decide on this costume," she asked grinning with her hands still wet from having reached into the ice chest.

"It was Vick's idea. He needed someone to be his other half," he said and nodded his green face in the direction towards the dance floor. Celeste turned to see Vick also dressed as half an avocado but without the seed. His half of the costume had the hole, and his face was painted green too. He wore green leg warmers over his tights.

"Oh my God," Celeste said and waved to Vick. She wondered where he found tights long enough to cover his lengthy limbs.

"Yeah, I told him I wouldn't be the hole. I said he had to be the hole," Bahn joked.

"Well, the seed does make it more manly," she said and smiled.

He rubbed the big brown seed popping out of his belly and asked, "Does it? Because I kind of feel like I'm pregnant with some sort of polyunsaturated baby." He went on, "Vick wanted to get a picture of me planting my seed in his hole, but I drew the line at that and said no. I told him it's too soon in our relationship, and we're not ready for that. But you! Look at you! You look like a Greek goddess." He couldn't take his eyes off her.

She laughed, winked at him and said, "Thanks, I was going for more of a peasant girl, but I could be talked into being a goddess." It must be the alcohol winking, she thought. She heard 'You make me want to shout' playing in the background. Maybel insisted the D.J. play only oldies.

At that moment, Mandy Vu bopped up to them. "Are you that cop that's been investigating all the deaths in the building?" Tiny Mandy dressed up as a very perky cheerleader. There were ribbons around her pig tailed hair, and Detective Bahn noticed her pleated skirt barely covered her apple bottom.

He held out a green gloved hand to shake hers and said, "Yes, that would be me. Detective Bahn at your service."

Mandy put both her hands on his hand, tilted her head to the side and didn't let go. "Great costume! Do you like avocado toast? I love avocado toast! I came over here because I've been meaning to talk to you. I have some concerns about the building," she said and pulled him away.

Celeste took the bottles of water back to Veronica who sat on a lawn chair off in the corner of the roof. "This is a nice spot to hang out," Celeste said as she sat down next to her and handed her a bottle of cold water.

"Ah, thanks. I was parched. You know, I can't keep up with Maybel. Look at her," Veronica said and pointed to where Maybel led the limbo contest showing how low she could go.

"And she has an advantage over everyone because she's so short," Celeste said.

Veronica sipped from her bottle. "True. Who was that hunk of an avocado you were talking to? Are you planning on making guacamole later?"

Celeste threw her head back and laughed. "Girl, please. I'm too old for that."

"No, you're not." Veronica sipped her water.

"Well, I don't have the time or the energy," Celeste protested.

"Sure you do…and he is totally your type," Veronica nudged and took another swig of her water.

"No, he's not my type," Celeste protested again.

"I've known you fifteen years. Yes, he's your type. He's every-body's type."

Celeste conceded and sighed. "Ugh…I hate that he's my type."

As Celeste sat in the lawn chair and looked up at the night sky, she could see some stars glowing. The breeze blew through her hair, and she had more than a little bit of a buzz on. Taking in the party, she felt glad she attended and happy to be sitting next to her best friend. It warmed her heart to see Maybel and Janet having a good time. Celeste knew losing their friend Alice took a toll on them. The crowd doubled in size since they'd arrived, and the party raged in full swing. Into the dry October night air, the Werewolves from a little place called London howled.

Billy Cheng and his wife Lily walked out of the penthouse. They dressed as the Mad Hatter and Alice in Wonderland. Billy who was already very tall, with a top hat on, seemed gigantic. Lily on the other hand was very petite and wore the smallest Al-ice in Wonderland costume Celeste ever saw. A baby blue bustier laced up the back of her body and she wore black panties with it. She also wore black and white striped tights and clear glass stripper heels.

"Wow," Celeste said.

Veronica said louder than she should have, "Dang! Somebody's going down the rabbit hole tonight!" Celeste wanted to shush her but laughed instead. Billy and Lily proceeded to walk around the party chatting everyone up. They were like royalty, but something about Billy's demeanor bugged Celeste. He acted like he owned the whole place. Celeste knew from Maybel that Billy only rented the penthouse from a real estate investor who bought it years ear-lier. But even if Billy had owned the penthouse, he certainly didn't own the rooftop observation deck.

Tom Fitzpatrick approached Celeste and Veronica and asked Veronica if she wanted to dance. When she agreed, he extended one buffalo plaid covered arm to her to help her out of her chair. Celeste's heart felt full as her friend walked out to the dance floor with him. Tom did the robot, and Veronica followed suit. With beer in hand, Vick did some sort of shimmy behind them. The limbo contest seemed to be over, and Maybel raised her hands in the air like she just didn't care. Some folks bobbed for apples and came up out of the water with wet heads triumphantly clinching fruit in their teeth. No way would Celeste do that. She'd spent too much time on her hair and make-up. The clear sky made Celeste want to look out the telescope. She carefully got out of the lawn chair and made her way over to it, a bit wobbly from the booze.

She heard someone call her name and turned to see Detective Bahn again. "Brian, is Mandy all set?"

"Who? Oh, her? I guess. I have no idea what she was saying. Something about the environment and safe water for the dolphins and how avocados are one of the healthiest fats you can eat." He shook his avocado head.

"I was just about to look out the telescope. It's one of my favorite things about the building," Celeste said and bent down a little to peer up at the sky through the lens. As she star gazed, a party goer tripped into Detective Bahn, pushing him forward a bit. He brushed into Celeste's rear end. She straightened up, looked behind her, and asked, "Did you just bump me…with your seed?"

"Sorry. This costume is a little front heavy," Bahn said apologizing.

She pointed to the telescope and said, "Take a look."

He bent down and looked out the lens. "Spectacular!"

"Yeah, isn't it beautiful? It's like a map to the heavens. It's almost a full moon too," she said.

A song about a ball and chain rocked the air. It reminded Detective Bahn of his youthful indiscretions. When he was younger, he was a slave to his libido and that led to some bad decisions. As he grew older, he thought marriage would make him happy, but he messed that up too. His good looks made him a walking temptation to women. As the song continued to plead for something better, Detective Bahn felt the hope in it. During the next song, he finally got up the nerve and suggested to Celeste, "We should go dance under the moonlight."

Mandy bounced back over, yanked on his arm and said, "There you are! We need you for the conga line!"

Celeste grinned from ear to ear. Amused at the thought of seeing him in a conga line dressed up as a California avocado she said, "They need you. You better go." Bahn's face looked pained, but Celeste kept smiling.

Mandy thought Detective Bahn looked like a superhero and couldn't keep her hands off him. She dragged him off to the conga line as a new song played.

Celeste sat back down on her lawn chair and watched everyone parade around. Maybel kicked her legs out at the front of the conga line like a pied piper. Celeste snapped off a few photos of it. One of the tenants made balloon animals for the children, and another tenant led a game of pin the tail on the donkey. Celeste remembered the joke Maybel made saying the game should be called pin the tail on Vick.

After the conga line died down, Celeste heard some people shouting somewhere on the roof, "Chug! Chug! Chug!" Later, when they gave out prizes for the best costumes, Maybel announced Vick and Detective Bahn won best couple's costume. Billy and Lily looked a little disappointed they didn't win.

Veronica rushed back to Celeste's side breathless from her dancing. "Hey, that Tom guy is kind of cute, huh?"

"He seems like a nice guy," Celeste replied.

"If you don't mind, I'm going to go back to his place," Veronica said.

"I don't mind. Please be careful. Call me if you need anything. And text me when you leave…and when you get home."

"Yes Mom," Veronica teased and gave her hug. Tom waited at the exit for her.

Celeste waited a few minutes more and decided to slip out behind them and go back to her condo. It was getting late, she was tired, cold, and she had enough to drink. Nothing good ever happens after midnight anyway, she thought.

When she got inside her condo, she realized her ears were ringing from the music, and her feet were throbbing. She took off her gold leaf crown, set it down on the coffee table, and slipped out of her sandals. She only meant to lay there for a few minutes, but in the morning, she was still on the couch. The sun streamed in from the windows. She felt thirsty and her head throbbed a little. She smiled to herself remembering the fun night.

She also remembered Veronica went home with Tom. She jumped up and checked her phone. Around 1 a.m. there was a text from her: **Hung out with Tom for a while. He was a perfect gentleman. Leaving now to go home.**

After that text, there was another text from her at 1:30 a.m.: **I made it home safe. Good night!**

Some friend I am. I slept through both of those texts, Celeste thought. She made her way to her room, took off her costume and hopped in the shower putting her hair up before she got in—no need to wash it yet. After that, she got into a pair of sweats and a t-shirt and headed into the kitchen to get a cup of coffee. But first, she drank a big glass of water for her slight hang over.

Around 10 a.m. Maybel knocked at her door. Celeste offered some coffee. "No thanks. I already had some along with an aspirin," she said. They both sat down on her couch and Celeste sipped from her mug while her head pounded.

Celeste praised Maybel for her efforts and said, "Well, that was a fun night. What a great party. You and the committee did a fantastic job!"

"Yeah, I think it turned out pretty good. I had fun, but I went home with someone else's leg warmers."

Celeste chuckled and asked, "Janet's?"

Maybel rubbed her temples and said, "I have no idea who's they are…or where mine are. I had a bit to drink last night. I did one of those beer bangs."

"You mean beer bong? It's called a beer bong," Celeste corrected her quickly.

"I don't know. It was a skulls head with a tube on it, and they poured a beer down it."

"I'm glad you had a good time. Your costume was great," Celeste said and smiled.

"You know, back in the day, I used to really do aerobics. I needed to stay in shape for George because—"

"Nope, no. I got it. You don't need to tell me," Celeste interrupted. "It was nice to see Jeffrey again," Celeste said changing the subject.

"Yeah, but I don't think his new girlfriend is really a nun like he said. Her skirt was much too short. I told him I still expect grandkids, and then he told me he took a vow of silence and couldn't discuss it anymore," Maybel said seeming annoyed at the memory of the conversation with her son.

Celeste smiled.

"When did you leave the party? You didn't say goodbye. Poor Detective Bahn was looking for you," Maybel said and waited for Celeste's answer.

"Oh, I don't know. Maybe just before midnight. I left right after Veronica left."

"So you wouldn't turn in to a pumpkin?"

"Exactly," Celeste answered.

"Well, that Mandy really pasted herself to him…wouldn't leave his side the whole night," Maybel went on, "You left before he started break dancing. You should have seen his seed spinning around when he was on his back on the dance floor! He also did the Macarena, but at the point in the night, his seed was hanging kind of low."

Celeste chuckled along with Maybel…neither of them were aware what lurked ahead for Regal Palms.

Chapter Thirteen

Go Green

The dry October wind blew fiercely hot in Sunshine Beach. Celeste got ready for work quickly, and because of the heat, she did a French braid with her long wavy hair. She picked out a light-weight orange summer dress embroidered with yellow and red flowers. She applied orange lip gloss and bronzy glow powder making her cheeks look radiantly sun kissed. She slipped into her beige wedge heels and slipped out the door.

As usual, she got slammed from 9 a.m. on. Since it was too hot to go outside, so she didn't take a lunch break. She ate the snack she brought with her and plugged along the best she could. When it was quittin' time, she bolted out of the office and hit the road. It was time for another HOA Board meeting, and Maybel made her promise to go with her. After fighting traffic, parking in the underground structure in her reserved spot, and riding up the creaky elevator to her condo, she made a quick dinner of salmon and asparagus. She just finished washing dishes when Maybel knocked at her door.

Celeste helped Maybel carry her homemade cupcakes and a big jug of fruit punch down to the Rec room. After setting it out on a side table, Maybel wanted to say hello to all the board members. Celeste bowed out and took a seat. Residents filtered in, and she suspected it would be standing room only again. Three people died over the summer, which was almost unbelievable. Celeste looked in Maybel's direction and saw her arguing with Vick. She could only read their body language, but it seemed hostile. Vick finally waved his hand in a gesture for her to leave. Maybel thumped down on her seat next to Celeste.

Celeste asked, "What was that about?"

Maybel went off like a little firecracker. "He's an asshole! That's what that was about. I let him know what I think he did, and he told me that I'm crazy, but I'm not crazy. And even if I was crazy, how would he know? Because he's crazy! And crazy can't identify crazy. He's let the power of the presidency go to his bald, comb-over head!"

People continued to filter into the room until all the seats were taken. Vick banged his gavel aggressively. More people piled into the back of the room and had to stand. "Order! Order!" Vick shouted.

Someone in the crowd shouted back, "This isn't a court room, Vick." Laughter followed that, and Celeste hadn't heard Maybel laugh like that in a while. It was nice to hear her laugh again. Celeste knew Alice's death landed hard on Maybel.

Vick banged the gavel like he was teaching it a lesson. He spoke sternly, "This meeting will begin." For good measure, he banged once more.

Celeste looked around the room and saw Detective Brian Bahn leaning against the wall. She wondered why he attended the meeting again. Vick began, "Good evening, everyone. We know that many of you are aware there have been a few accidents here at Regal Palms. We don't have an official agenda for tonight's meeting. We, the board, wanted to let you know the problem in the laundry room was looked at. The upgrade to the electrical is almost done."

A man in a UCLA t-shirt and jeans shouted a question, "But what about the lady that drowned in the pool?"

Vick looked flustered. "We believe that was an accident too. We have no reason to believe otherwise," Vick said. That prompted a lot of chatter around the room. Celeste thought either Vick was lying to keep everyone calm, or Detective Bahn hadn't told the board what he'd told her. Vick banged his gavel again. "The electrician is working on the electrical in the laundry room, and as most of you know, right now it is closed. After we've been assured everything is ok, we'll open it again."

Alex Graham asked, "What are we supposed to do about our laundry in the meantime?"

Angie Adams said, "We apologize for the inconvenience, but for the time being, you will need to go to a laundry mat. We sent out a letter about this. There is one around the corner form here. We just need to put everyone's safety first." That prompted more grumbling in the room.

Celeste wished she skipped the meeting. The room got stuffy, and everyone seemed on edge. After more discussion about the safety of the laundry room, pool, roof, lack of parking, the elevator that stalls, and trash shoots getting backed up, Vick asked if there were any more questions.

Mandy Vu stood up and raised her hand eagerly. Vick nodded his head at her. She spoke in a perky demeanor like the meeting was a pep rally, "Yeah, hi! My name is Mandy Vu, and I've lived in this building for a few years. I was just wondering if Regal Palms will ever consider going green? I noticed that there is no system for recycling and no way to separate our trash that goes down the trash shoot. I mean, this just isn't right for the environment. We really need to go green. Gooooooo green!"

Celeste was pretty sure Mandy was a democrat. While listening to Mandy speak about plastic and recyclables, Celeste agreed she made some good points. It was true that Regal Palms didn't have a system for recycling. Due to the age of the building, it still housed a very old-fashioned trash shoot. From time to time, it got clogged up. The smell from that was disgusting. Celeste looked over at Detective Bahn, and he smiled at her.

Tom Fitzpatrick, another board member who reminded Celeste of a bulldog, interrupted cute little Mandy. "Young lady, we've told you before we don't have enough money in the special assessment fund to add a second trash shoot to the building to recycle. At this time, it is not possible. This is a very old building and is always in need of a lot of maintenance."

More chatter from the room erupted and some other hands went up with questions about additional building issues.

When one neighbor complained about another neighbor's dog, Celeste hit her limit. She leaned over and said in Maybel's ear, "I'm going back up to my place. I'm tired."

Maybel nodded at her. "Ok honey, I'll save you a cupcake."

Celeste squeezed past the people in the seats around her and walked out of the room. She did a fast stride through the lobby, and as she got about halfway to the elevator, she heard someone call her name. She turned to see Detective Bahn chasing after her. "Hello," she greeted him.

He asked, "Are those meetings always like that?"

"Yes, and I hate them…but I think you've been to almost as many board meetings as I have. I don't have the patience for them."

Bahn looked like he wanted to say something to her. Celeste tilted her head to the side and waited. He finally said, "I just…I want to remind you to be safe."

Celeste snapped, "Yeah, you told me that already." Then she realized he was trying to be nice. "I'm sorry. I don't mean to be rude. I'm just tired, and those meetings always get on my nerves. They're almost as bad as the meetings at work."

He put his hand on her arm and steered her towards the elevator. "I understand. Let me get the elevator for you." He hit the up arrow.

As they waited, Celeste asked, "How did you know where I lived? The first time you came to my condo…how did you find it?"

"Maybel made sure I knew where you lived," he said.

Celeste chuckled. Of course she did, she thought. "Will you do me a favor? After the meeting, will you walk Maybel to her place?"

"Sure. I gotta get back in there and answer some questions. The board asked me to help out." Bahn smiled at her right before the elevator door closed.

She smiled back as the door closed and let out a deep breath. Once in her pajamas, she watched an old 'Thin Man' movie. About an hour into the movie, she drifted off to sleep to Myrna Loy's dreamy half-moon lit eyes.

Mandy

Mandy Vu cheered for her high school's varsity cheerleading team and believed everything could be solved with a hug and a whole lot of tolerance. Her very liberal political views led her to believe it was a sin not to take care the environment. Her wealthy parents bought a condo for her. She wanted to live by the beach because she loved the ocean and the dolphins.

When she graduated from college, she knew she would change the world! She wanted to become an activist for global warming. The first place to start was right here at home. It was practically unforgivable that Regal Palms didn't recycle. She would get the board to approve a second trash shoot for recyclables if it was the last thing she did.

After a long day of writing energetically worded letters to big corporations that weren't as green as she believed they needed to be, Mandy tidied up her condo. She hadn't taken her trash out in a few days. That was the last chore she needed to do, and then she would relax in a nice hot bubble bath—with chemical free soap, of course. She pulled the bag out of her kitchen trash can and headed out to the hallway around 10:15 p.m.

She tugged on the cold brass handle of the trash shoot's door and lifted it up. She got a whiff of the old trash smell of rotten eggs and crinkled up her button nose. She couldn't see the trash at the end of the shoot. It was just an unrecycled smelly black hole. She dropped her bag down the shoot, again thinking what a tragedy it was that she couldn't recycle. She was just as sad about that as she would have been attending a loved one's funeral.

As she closed the trash shoot door, she heard the faint noise of a plastic bag crinkling behind her. Before she could turn around, the bag slid over her head and clinched tight around her neck. She whipped from side to side in a panic. Her chest heaved. She kicked, bucked, and tried to pull back. She hit the ground breathing out and not able to breath in. Plastic breached the inside of her mouth and took the life right out of her. The recyclable bag stole all the air from Mandy…the good clean air from the environment she fought so hard to protect.

Chapter Fourteen

Into the Deep Blue Sea

The bus was going too fast, and Celeste didn't understand why no one else on the bus seemed concerned about the speed. As the bus driver turned the corner rounding the mountain road, he swerved too far to the left, which caused him to over correct by abruptly turning to the right. As he did, he lost control of the bus, and they went off the cliff straight down into the deep blue sea below. Celeste gripped the seat in front of her as hard as she could. She prayed for her life. Once again, she was thrust into the Pacific Ocean and came face to face with a hungry shark. She jolted awake and heard a sound—a knock on wood. Her heart pounded in her ears from her reoccurring stress dream. She heard an aggressive knock at her door again. She got out of bed and put on her slippers and robe. Her remodeled condo, with an industrial style concrete floor, was not the best to walk around barefoot on.

She checked the time, and it was 9:36 p.m. She walked down her hallway, turning on only the track lighting in the hall that illuminated her bookcases. She looked through the peep hole and saw Detective Brian Bahn. What the heck is he doing here?

She unlocked the door and opened it a crack. "Hey, what's going on?"

"May I come in? I need to speak with you," he said and before she could answer he pushed on the door. She stepped aside. He instantly got distracted by the view out the west windows. "Wow! I hadn't seen the view at night. It's like little diamonds in the sky!" He walked closer to the windows and stared out them. While he stood there lit by nothing but city lights, Celeste admired his silhouette. He possessed quite a strong physique. He turned and looked at her. As she stood before him in the moonlight, his eyes moved up and down her figure a few times.

She suddenly felt very self-conscious and aware she didn't have a bra on. She pulled her robe closed around her and cleared her throat. "What brings you here?"

There was judgement in his voice when he asked, "Were you asleep already?" He teased her and said, "You've been hanging out with the senior citizens too much."

"Actually, Maybel stays up a lot later than I do. She stays alert for some sort of phone tree. And I have to get up at 4:30 tomorrow morning," she stated defensively.

"I know Maybel stays up later than you do. I was just talking to her."

Celeste knew this wasn't good. "What's going on?"

"Mandy Vu was found suffocated and strangled in the trash bin. It looks like someone killed her and stuffed her down the trash shoot. She was found late this afternoon when they came to pick up the trash."

Celeste felt wobbly and needed to sit down. She collapsed onto the grey leather chair.

Detective Bahn moved closer to her and knelt down on one knee. His voice was calm. "Did you know her well?"

"Not really. I think she'd lived here a couple of years. I'd seen her around a few times, and she was at the last board meeting. I think she lives on the same floor as Tom Fitzpatrick and Vick Arnold, two of the board members."

Bahn replied, "Yes, that's what Maybel said. Another neighbor said they'd heard Mandy arguing with Tom about something."

"She was determined to get the board to approve putting in another trash shoot so that we could all recycle. She was so diligent for such a noble cause. I can't believe this…," Celeste said.

"Geez…that's right. Now I remember that from the meeting," Bahn said and sighed. He lowered his voice and went on, "Mandy was found with a plastic recyclable bag around her head. Someone choked and suffocated her with it. We're going to dust it for prints but if the killer wore gloves, then…"

"It will do no good," Celeste said and sat there in the dark with Bahn on his knee next to her. They looked intently at each other. Celeste's voice was barely audible. "This has gotten so out of control." She was breathing heavy. Her body was shaking. A panic attack? "I feel like I'm going to throw up," she said.

Detective Bahn patted her back to comfort her and said, "Hey…hey, it's going to be ok. Just breathe. Do you want a glass of water?"

"No." She took a few more deep breaths.

Bahn put his hand on her arm. "We're going to catch this killer," he assured her.

"What if it's not just one killer? What if these deaths aren't all related? What if the killer doesn't even live in the building? At first, I thought the killer had to live here, but if you really think about it, that could be an incorrect assumption. At one point, I even thought maybe Mark was the killer because he was kind of creepy, and Maybel said he lived next door to Jennifer. But now he's dead, and the murders keep happening!"

"I wish I had a better answer for you. We are working on this. The killer knows where there are no security cameras like the roof, laundry room, pool and hallways. It's been difficult because of the lack of physical evidence, but we are not about to give up. In the meantime, I need you to be extremely cautious. Keep your eyes and ears open. Let me know if you see or hear anything suspicious," he instructed.

"I will."

Bahn stood up and grabbed her hand and pulled her out of the chair towards him. "I have to get going. Come lock the door behind me," he said. She followed him to the door. "We've brought in both Tom and Vick for questioning. I'll keep you posted. Do you own a gun?"

"No."

He frowned. "Do you have a lock on your bedroom door?"

Celeste nodded.

"Use it," he said.

Celeste nodded and said goodbye to him. She locked the door after he left, turned out the hall lights, and went back to her bed. She locked her bedroom door. Celeste wondered how she would sleep after that. She decided to call Veronica.

Veronica sounded chipper. "Hello, what are you doing up this late?" Her friend knew her habits.

"Ronnie, I have to tell you something. There was a murder in the building. Mandy Vu was found strangled in the trash shoot," Celeste said, and her stomach was in knots.

"What? The cheerleader?"

"Yes. Someone killed her. They strangled her and shoved her down the trash shoot here at the building."

Veronica shrieked, "Oh God! That's horrible!"

"Yeah, but there's more. They took Tom Fitzpatrick in for questioning. Look, I know you like him, but—"

"Don't worry, Celeste. I barely know him. He has my cell and said he'd call so we could go out sometime, but I haven't heard from him yet. I'll be careful. I don't need a date that bad," Veronica said.

"Ok, good. I'm going to try to get some sleep now."

"Celeste, be careful," Veronica urged.

"I will be," Celeste reassured her.

Veronica asked, "Do you want to stay at my place?"

"No, I'll be ok. Thanks for the offer though," Celeste said appreciating her friend's concern.

After her call with Veronica, Celeste called Maybel. "I can't believe Mandy was found dead. This is out of control! It's absolute mayhem!"

"I know, dear. Keep your door locked," Maybel warned.

"I will, and you do the same."

Maybel said, "Oh, I will, and I have George's gun beside me too."

Celeste tossed and turned for a long time. Her mind raced picturing what happened to Mandy. That poor girl had her whole life ahead of her. Who is doing this? And why? Eventually, she fell back asleep. Sometime around 2 a.m., she woke up from another nightmare. She was in the deep blue sea again with a shark's mouth coming towards her. It startled her awake, and she sat up in her bed. She could have sworn someone jiggled her bedroom doorknob, but she convinced herself it was part of the dream. She heard Birino's cage squeak. She told herself she was just paranoid and laid back down. She did some more deep breathing until she drifted back to sleep.

Chapter Fifteen

BFFs

Detective Brian Bahn interrogated numerous suspects before. Treat a suspect like they are guilty until they confess. It worked most of the time. Tom Fitzpatrick sat on a cold metal chair across the table from him. They were in a small room with double mirrors, with no one on the other side. Tom sat defiantly looking back at Detective Bahn. He'd been a military man and knew the drill.

"Mr. Fitzpatrick, we've already established that you were seen and heard arguing with the victim, Mandy Vu. We know she sent you and other board members threatening emails. We know you responded in a less than friendly manner, and we know you don't have an alibi for the night she was murdered. We've also already spoken with Vick Arnold. This will go much easier for you if you just tell us the truth." Bahn sat, waited, and wouldn't speak again until Tom spoke.

Tom said calmly, "I didn't do anything."

"Are you denying you had an argument with Mandy the day she was killed?"

"No, I had an argument with her," Tom confirmed.

Bahn asked, "Why don't you tell me what you two argued about?"

"She wanted the board to approve putting in a second trash shoot for recycling. She was bugging us relentlessly about it," Tom said and let out a disgusted sigh.

Bahn goaded him and asked, "That doesn't seem like a big deal. Why would you argue with her about that?"

"Look, everyone that lives in that building has an opinion about what they think the board members should do, but none of them want to spend their time serving on the board dealing with the problems, nor do any of them want their HOA dues increased to pay for all the things they demand," Tom said and stared at Bahn.

"I still don't see why this would need to turn into an argument," Bahn continued to goad Tom.

"It shouldn't have, but she wouldn't let it go. She was obsessed with it and getting unreasonable. She threatened us with legal action, and she'd even looked into the board members' backgrounds." Tom let some information slip without meaning to.

Bahn already looked into all of the board members backgrounds and knew the answer when he asked, "Did she find out about your domestic abuse charge?"

Tom felt flustered for a second, regained his composure and asked, "Yeah. So?"

"Might have made you angry, and we know you have trouble controlling your temper. In one of your emails to Mandy, you told her to…and I quote 'why don't you go choke on a plastic bottle'," Bahn said pushing his point forward. He tapped his pen on the notepad in front of him.

"It was just an expression, and I didn't do anything to that girl. She was annoying, but I didn't lay a hand on her. And what happened with my ex-wife was a long time ago. It was part of my PTSD. It has nothing to do with this," Tom stated clearly.

Bahn continued to prod Tom for a while but got nowhere. He'd also gotten nowhere with Vick but wasn't going to let either of them know how it went with the other one.

Tom's patience was running out and he asked, "Are you going to charge me with something or am I free to go?"

Bahn still didn't feel he had enough physical evidence. One threat does not make a murderer. He hated to let him go, but he had no other evidence for the other murders in the building. Tom had an alibi for Alice and Mark's murders. But maybe these deaths weren't all connected. Bahn reluctantly let Tom go and warned him not to leave town.

When back at his desk, Detective Bahn looked through all the case notes again. Two hours into that, the Chief of Police knocked on his door. "Enter," he called out.

They called the police chief Dan. Chief Daniel Rivers. He'd been a beat cop for many years, then detective, then got promoted to Chief last year. Dan was surprised as anyone when he was promoted. He thought the job would go to the mayor's good buddy. Now that Dan had the job, he pretty much hated it. He missed being a detective and got tired of riding the guys for whatever was on the mayor's list.

Chief Rivers stood in the doorway. "This Regal Palms case—you got this? It's getting a lot of attention in the news. You need any help with it?"

Detective Bahn took a sip from his cold and bitter cup of coffee. He was savvy enough to know the Chief wasn't asking. "Sure, if you want to put a second set of eyes on the file that would be great."

"You didn't make an arrest tonight," Chief Rivers said.

Detective Bahn took in a long breath. "No, I didn't. In my gut I don't think it's Tom Fitzpatrick even though he made a threat."

"What about the other guy? The greasy one," the Chief asked.

"No evidence," Bahn said and felt defeated.

He remembered the hurt look on Vick's face when he questioned him. Bahn was too guarded to be affected by it, but it did seem genuine. Bahn tried as hard as he could, but he couldn't get Vick to crack either.

"I thought we were friends," Vick said with a wounded look in his eyes. "We even dressed alike at the Halloween party…"

To Vick that meant they were best friends. To Detective Bahn it was just a way to get closer to Celeste.

Chapter Sixteen

Sweet Cherry Pie

The Saturday after Mandy's death it was Celeste's turn to make lunch for her and Maybel. She planned to use a new recipe she'd read in a murder mystery book for tuna melts. Instead of a spoonful of mayonnaise mixed with the canned tuna, it called for onion dip from sour cream and dried onion soup mix. She combined the onion dip with the tuna and put tomatoes and Swiss cheese over the tops. She stuck them under the broiler until the cheese got bubbly. Celeste limited her dairy intake to only once a week, and this was it.

Maybel said they were delicious. Celeste also served Maybel two scoops of mango sorbet for dessert, along with their coffee. "The only ice cream I ever kept in the house was Neapolitan. That's all George ever wanted," Maybel said as she enjoyed her fruity sweet treat. Celeste smiled at her. It was nice Maybel got to a point where she could reminisce about George without breaking down and crying. "Who do you think has been bumping everyone off?"

"I really don't know, and I'm not sure all the murders have been done by the same person…and it could be possible that the murderer doesn't even live in this building. All I know is we need to be careful. Detective Bahn made a good point the other day. He said the murderer or murderers seem to know where the security cameras are and aren't. You know like the roof, hallways, pool and laundry room don't have cameras," Celeste said.

"You've been talking to Detective Bahn?" Maybel asked with a grin on her face.

Celeste knew what Maybel was getting at. "He stopped by the night they found Mandy Vu. He had some questions for me."

Maybel kept grinning. "Oh, I see, so that's all it was?"

Celeste sipped her coffee. "I know he stopped by to talk to you too."

"I'm convinced it's Vick. I told him as much at the last board meeting too," Maybel said.

Celeste said, "I know, I remember. Imagine if it was Vick… and Detective Bahn dressed as an avocado with him. Detective Bahn must not think it's Vick."

"Maybe it is a far-fetched idea. I just feel so unsafe here now," Maybel said and wrung her hands. Celeste knew how much this troubled her. It desperately troubled them both. "When Jeffrey heard about Mandy, he insisted on getting me a cell phone and showing me how to use it. He said I need to keep the phone with me at all times no matter where I go in the building. He also showed me how to send texts." Maybel gave Celeste her knew cell number, and Celeste punched it into her phone.

Maybel hung out a little while longer, and they continued to chat over coffee. Celeste wasn't convinced it was Vick, but she wanted to reach out to Detective Bahn to see how things were going. After Maybel left, Celeste cleaned up her condo and paid some bills. It was also time to pay the monthly HOA dues again. She took her check downstairs and checked the bulletin board. Not much was new. Someone thumb tacked a take-out menu from a local Chinese restaurant to the board. Kung Pao Chicken…yum.

She walked into the property management office and saw Janice's friendly face. "Hi Celeste," she chirped at her with a smile. "It's always a pleasure to see you."

"Hey, how are you?" Celeste really liked Janice and thought she did a good job.

Janice looked up from her computer screen. "Not too bad for a Saturday. It's been pretty quiet. I think everyone is freaked out about that young gal Mandy. So scary! I heard she'd been writing threatening letters to both Tom and Vick because they refused to put in a second trash shoot for recycling."

"Yeah, I heard that too. But I can't imagine anything came of that," Celeste said reasoning it.

"Then who could have done that to her?" Janice went on, "I mean, the other deaths could have been accidents or a suicide, but there is no way Mandy's death was an accident or suicide!"

Celeste kept silent. Detective Bahn told her about some things in confidence, and she didn't want to betray his trust. She also knew that none of the deaths were accidents or a suicide.

"And that hot police detective questioned all of the board members. It looks suspicious. Do you know that since Mandy's death, at least five homeowners have listed their condos for sale? And two renters just gave notice they are moving out…everyone wants out."

Celeste took a deep breath and said, "I can't blame them. This isn't normal. Just promise me you'll be careful, Janice."

Janice grabbed her purse and pulled out a can of pepper spray. "Oh, I will," she said and held it up proudly.

Celeste warned, "If you ever use that stuff, don't breathe it in."

Janice laughed and asked, "On another note, how fun was that Halloween party?"

"So fun! I didn't see you there. What were you dressed as?"

"I was dressed up as a Marti Gras party goer. I had a mask on," Janice winked and added, "…and a whole lot of beads."

"Ah, I see. The mask must have been why I missed you."

"Oh, by the way, I have something to show you," Janice said and bent down. She pulled out a big cardboard box marked 'lost and found'. She took a pen and reached into the box. She hooked the pen through the leg of a pair of black panties and held them up. "These were turned into the lost and found after the party. They were found on the roof. Are they yours?"

Celeste laughed and leaned back away from them. "Geez no! Looks like it really was a fun party for everyone."

"Yeah, for sure. Vick was also in here earlier to find out if anyone turned in some green leg warmers that went with his avocado costume, but I told him no one had turned them in yet," Janice held up a pair of pink leg warmers and said, "He turned these in."

Celeste smiled knowing who had the green ones. "Have a good evening, Janice. I'll see you later," Celeste said and left the property management office. She walked through the lobby and over to the mailboxes. As she was digging her mail out of the slot, she heard the clickity clack of heels on the lobby tiles. She got a whiff of a sickeningly sweet, musky perfume. Vanilla with a hint of sandalwood? She turned and noticed Lily Cheng standing by one of the rows of mailboxes, staring at them blankly. Celeste greeted her and moved a little closer.

"Oh hi! I always forget which box is ours," Lily said and laughed a high-pitched squeal. Celeste tried not to wince. She noticed Lily's outfit. It would have been difficult not too. Tight cut off denim shorts were a little ripped up and clinging to her curves. A red tube top was stretched to the limit across her ample bosom, and red heels propped her calves up. Her ratted and teased hair gave it more height. Scarlet painted lips jumped off her face. She could have been plucked right out of a 1980's heavy metal band video.

Celeste pointed up and smiled. "I think yours is towards the top row since you live in the penthouse."

"You're right. There it is!" Lily reached up toward it to unlock it, and as she did, more of her butt cheeks peaked out from under her shorts.

As Lily collected her mail, Celeste decided to make the most of this opportunity and ask Lily some questions. "Terrible about that gal that jumped off the roof, huh?"

Lily froze for a second. She looked at Celeste and said, "Yeah, I guess so."

"I think she used to sunbathe on the observation deck a lot. Did you ever happen to see her?"

Lily stared at Celeste for a few seconds and then spoke carefully, "Yes, many times."

Celeste asked, "Were you friends with her?"

Lily snorted a half laugh and replied, "No, absolutely not!"

Well at least she's being honest, Celeste thought. "Had she done something to upset you?"

Lily clutched her mail close to her chest and let out a sigh. "That slut used to take her top off and sunbathe in the nude on the roof in front of my husband! I told her several times that was inappropriate and asked her to stop. Look, I'm not ashamed of the human body or anything like that, but my husband Billy is just a man. His flesh is weak, you know? You can't put temptation in front of a man like that," Lily said.

"No, I don't suppose you can. I can't believe she did that," Celeste said hoping to gain Lily's trust by sympathizing with her.

"She was like a cat in heat! I almost turned the hose on her one day when I went out to the roof to water my victory garden and found her sitting there topless. She gave me some BS about not wanting tan lines, and I told her I didn't give a shit about her tan lines," Lily went on, "And do you know what else she did? She got a hold of my husband's number and started texting him. She sent him some nude photos of herself! If you ask me, she was just a gold digger," Lily said.

Celeste nodded her head. "I think you're right. How did you find out she'd been texting your husband?"

"I went through his phone one night. I'm not proud of that, but you gotta keep tabs on your man, you know? Especially when they are as rich and good looking as Billy is," Lily said.

Celeste asked, "Do you think Billy had an affair with her?"

"No, I know he didn't. They had just started texting before I intercepted it. He swears they didn't do anything. Not that she didn't try. If you ask me, I'm glad she's gone," Lily said.

I'll bet, Celeste thought and pushed a little more. "You know, I heard a rumor that the cops think she was murdered."

Lily slammed her mailbox shut. "Wouldn't surprise me a bit. A woman like that had to have had a lot of enemies."

"Were you home the morning she jumped off the roof?" Celeste felt guilty for lying. She knew Jennifer hadn't jumped.

"Look, I'll tell you what I told the police when they questioned us. Billy and I were together that morning, and we weren't home. Neither one of us had anything to do with Jennifer's death," she said.

"Oh, I'm sorry. I didn't mean to imply anything. It's just with you up in the penthouse, I know you have a clear view of the whole observation deck. I was wondering if you saw anything suspicious," Celeste said.

"No, not really. Like I said to the police, we weren't home."

Celeste wanted to ask where they had been, but knew it wasn't her job to. She did have one more question for Lily. "The day of the art festival over on Lansing Street, my friend and I saw you and Billy there."

"Yeah, we were there," Lily said.

"Well, I know it's none of my business, but it appeared you two were fighting about something. I saw him grab you and shake you. I was a little worried. Was everything ok?"

Lily broke eye contact and looked down at her shoes. "He was mad at me. He bought me that new beamer and told me not to park in the far corner of the lot across the street. It's too dark in that corner. But one night there was nowhere else to park, so I parked there. Then later someone tried to break into the car. Billy was angry all day about it. He doesn't like to be disobeyed," Lily said.

Celeste felt bad for Lily and said, "You know, if you ever need help with anything or someone to talk to, please know you can reach out to me."

"I could—"

"Lily!" Just then Billy appeared in the lobby. Both Lily and Celeste turned to look at him. He looked annoyed. Billy ordered, "Come, let's go!" Lily turned on a heel and walked away towards him. Celeste locked her mailbox and stalled for a minute or two. The last thing she wanted to do was ride up in the elevator with them.

Back at her place, Celeste locked her front door and checked it a second time. At least being on the ninth floor she didn't have to worry about anyone breaking in through a window. She had the whole rest of her Saturday afternoon open. As she wondered how it went for Detective Bahn when he questioned Vick and Tom, she heard her phone bing. She looked at it and had a text from him. Speak of the devil, she thought. It read: **Questioned Arnold and Fitzpatrick. Neither have an alibi for the night of Mandy's murder, and both deny any wrongdoing. We still have no hard evidence on anyone. No prints on the bag.**

Nothing really came of those leads she thought. She texted back: **Thanks for the update**

Celeste went into her office and said hello to Birino and watched him splash around a little in the bird bath inside his cage. She looked at the painting hanging on the wall above her desk. It depicted a Paris street scene on a rainy day. Every time she looked at it, she wished she could walk into that painting and walk down that street. She sat down at her desk and checked her emails. Then she moved her laptop to the side and pulled out a pad of drawing paper. As she stared at the blank paper, she tried to imagine what she wanted to put on it. Drawing relieved stress for her as it occupied her mind. She got out her set of pencils and begin to sketch the Regal Palms building. Normally she wouldn't use a ruler when she drew, but for this it seemed necessary.

After about thirty minutes of sketching, she'd drawn the building. It was a bit tedious. She also sketched a palm tree along the street and two people standing on the sidewalk. She sat back from the drawing feeling quite pleased with it. She took her pastel chalk out of her desk drawer and added some color to it. She lost track of time until her stomach started to growl. "Dinner time," she said to Birino and stood up to stretch her back and legs. She put on a Sam Cooke record. She loved the crackling sound the needle made when it hit the vinyl.

She went into the kitchen, preheated the oven and washed and cut up some Brussels sprouts. She placed them on a cookie sheet, poured a little olive oil over them, and added some salt and pepper. She mixed it up to incorporate it all the way through. She took a small steak out of the fridge to get the chill off it. She popped the Brussels sprouts in the oven and seasoned the steak.

Once the vegetables roasted for a good ten minutes, she heated up the skillet for her steak. She cooked it at a very high heat with lots of butter. The steak finished resting by the time the vegetables were done. She liked a little char on the Brussel sprouts and how some of the leaves turned into crispy little chips. She sat at her bar and ate dinner.

Back in her office, she looked at the picture she'd drawn earlier as Sam Cooke sang about Cupid. She liked the drawing but wished she could make it better. She always thought that about everything she drew. The building was old but possessed a certain type of charm to it. She thought she'd at least captured that in the drawing. Who would have thought back in 1958 when they built this building, that four people would be murdered? She got that chill again.

She shook her head and went into her bedroom. She locked the bedroom door and turned on the old movie channel. Another Noir film entertained her as she tried to keep her mind off what happened in the building. The movie started out with a sleepy train ride and made her wish she could get on one and go somewhere far away. If she could go back in time and star in one of these movies, she wouldn't even care if a gangster called her a broad, even though she'd prefer to be a dame who kept her fancy hats in decorative boxes. She snuggled into her bed a little more and eventually drifted off to sleep while a glamourous actress wearing a silky gown sang a sappy love song in a swanky nightclub.

Chapter Seventeen

The Murder Board

A few weeks went by after Mandy's murder and took them into November. Celeste kept herself busy at work making sure she met her end of the year deadlines. She never waited until the last minute to do things that could be done ahead of time. Around mid-month while she was finalizing some claims, she received a text from Maybel that read: **Do you have a whiteboard at your work?**

Celeste: **Yes**

Maybel: **Can you borrow it and bring it home tonight?**

Celeste: **Yes, why?**

Maybel: **Don't worry about that now. Bring some erasable markers and those stick-its**

Celeste: **Do you mean post-its?**

Maybel: **Yes, see you tonight. Snacks will be provided**

Celeste continued to plow through her paperwork. She was interrupted by phone calls and emails only twelve more times before the day was done. She went into the conference room and grabbed the whiteboard tucked behind a cabinet. It was rarely used and a bit dusty. She also borrowed a pack of markers and some post-its and headed out.

She felt pretty sure she knew what Maybel wanted to do, and Celeste was on the same page with the idea. She pulled her car into her parking spot and slid the whiteboard out of the back seat. She lugged it through the underground parking lot and gingerly got in the elevator with it. Since Maybel texted snacks would be provided, she decided to go straight to Maybel's and didn't stop at her place to change and eat dinner.

Maybel set out trays of food in her second bedroom. She converted it to a den after Jeffrey moved out. Decorated with warm colors, the den had a cozy love seat and coffee table in the corner of the room. A tall lamp, magazine rack, and Maybel's knitting basket were at one end of the couch. A plush reading chair covered in plaid fabric sat on the other side. A beautiful still life painting hung on the wall across from the couch, a Mother's Day gift from her son Jeffrey. He loved to paint in his spare time. Maybel also set up Jeffrey's old easel, and Celeste knew to put the whiteboard on it. She set the markers and post-its on the coffee table next to some other random items. With her stomach growling, she picked up a little paper plate and filled it with snacks.

Maybel laid out a lovely charcuterie board complete with Italian cold cuts, nuts, cheeses, olives, crackers and veggies. She also set out a tray of fruit, dried fruit and Italian cookies from a deli that was George's favorite. Celeste was still stacking cold cuts and veggies on her plate when Janet showed up. "Now we can get started. Janet, please get some snacks," Maybel instructed her. Janet sat down on the love seat next to Celeste and dished up.

Maybel popped a dried apricot in her mouth and grabbed an erasable marker. "Ladies, I invited you here tonight because we need to take matters into our own hands. While I'm sure Detective Bahn is working very hard to find the murderer, he doesn't seem to be getting anywhere. I think we have to help him solve this."

"I agree," Janet said crunching on a carrot stick.

"I'm not sure this is going to do any good, but I'm willing to keep an open mind," Celeste said and ate a rolled-up piece of mortadella.

Maybel nodded, pointed to Celeste and said, "That's the right attitude to have. Now, let's get started." She pulled the cap off a marker and walked over to the whiteboard. At the top left-hand corner of the board, she wrote "**VICTIMS**" and underlined it.

Under the word victims, she drew a stick figure with two big circles underneath the arms of it and wrote "Jennifer" under the drawing.

Celeste asked, "What is that? What are you drawing?"

"This is Jennifer, remember dear? The girl who supposedly jumped off the roof, but we suspect there might have been foul play," Maybel explained.

"Yeah, I know who Jennifer is, but what are those circles on her?"

Maybel put a dot in the middle of each circle and said, "Those are her breasts, dear. She used her breasts as a weapon."

Celeste scolded, "Maybel, it's 2017. You are not supposed to slut shame anyone."

Maybel crunched up her nose and said, "Dear, I don't know what that means, but that sounds really messy."

"Ok, let's just move on," Celeste suggested.

Maybel picked up a nice photo of her friend Alice from the table and taped it to the whiteboard next to Jennifer. She wrote "Alice" under the photo. She also grabbed an extension cord and hung it over the whiteboard with the prong part of it lining up next to the photo of Alice. The cord was to represent Mark who was electrocuted in the laundry room. Maybel wrote "Mark" under the cord. After that, she drew another plain stick figure with pig tails and wrote "Mandy" under it.

With all four victims lined up on the left side of the board, Maybel drew a line vertically down the middle of the board and wrote "**SUSPECTS**" on the right side of the board. She drew another stick figure with three little lines coming out of the head under the word suspects.

Janet asked, "Who is that?"

"That's Vick," Maybel answered.

Celeste asked, "What are those lines on his head?"

"It's that idiot's comb-over," Maybel continued, "You know, he acts like he has a full head of hair, but I assure you, he doesn't."

"Alright, let's just stay focused on the task at hand," Celeste said.

Maybel wrote "Vick" under his stick figure and taped a tiny American flag next to it.

Janet ate a green olive and asked, "What is that for?"

"That represents Tom Fitzpatrick, the war vet," Maybel explained and wrote "Tom" under the flag.

Janet asked, "Ok, are these two our only suspects?"

"I think Billy Cheng might be another suspect," Celeste answered.

"I'm way ahead of you," Maybel said and taped a dollar bill next to the American flag to represent Billy and wrote "Billy" under the dollar. "Do you think we should also list his wife Lily as a suspect? I can draw more boobs."

Celeste said, "No, no we have plenty of boobs on the board already. Let's take these one at a time…starting with Jennifer. What would she have had in common with Vick, Tom and Billy?"

"Dear, I think you know she intercoursed with all of them," Maybel said.

Celeste asked, "How the heck would I know that? Are you sure she was also with Tom?"

"I have it on good sources that Jennifer slept with most of the fifth floor, and Vick and Tom both live on the fifth floor," Maybel explained.

Janet bristled.

Celeste asked, "And Billy?"

Maybel further explained, "I also have it on good sources that Jennifer sunbathed topless on the roof in clear sight of Billy's penthouse."

"But that doesn't mean her and Billy actually had sex," Celeste said.

"Dear, don't be naïve. Of course they did," Maybel said.

"Why wouldn't they have?" Janet said seeming a little annoyed, and Celeste wasn't sure why.

"Ok, so let's just assume all three of these men did have some sort of sexual intercourse with Jennifer. That is still not a motive for murder. And what would the connection between these men and Alice be?" Celeste asked.

"I'm glad you asked that," Maybel said. "Vick hated that Alice relentlessly bugged him about fixing the pool. She told me that one time he shouted at her."

"Still doesn't seem like a motive for murder," Celeste said.

"And what about Mark? What would any of these suspects have to do with Mark? And Mandy?" Janet grabbed a cracker and put a piece of cheese on it.

"I'll get to Mark later, but as for Mandy, we know for a fact that she was writing threatening letters to both Vick and Tom," Maybel said.

"Ok…is there any connection between Billy and Mandy?" Celeste ate a piece of salami.

Maybel answered, "Not that I can think of. There is a connection between Vick and at least three of the victims: Jennifer, Alice and Mandy…all roads lead back to Vick. Also, on the day of Jennifer's murder, I know for a fact that my phone tree didn't call Vick right away, yet when I was in the elevator on the way down to the street and he got in, he already knew about it! There would be no way he knew unless he was the murderer!"

Celeste frowned. "How do you know the phone tree didn't call him?"

"The people of Regal Palms are very loyal to me, dear. I get called first. Vick gets called last. By the time they got around to calling him, he didn't answer," Maybel explained.

Celeste pointed out someone outside the phone tree could have told him.

Janet asked, "Could one of these suspects have found out that the other men slept with Jennifer and gotten jealous?"

"Well, yeah, but then wouldn't they have murdered one or more of the suspects and not the victims?" Maybel asked.

"I don't think we are getting anywhere," Celeste said and grabbed a handful of salty almonds.

"Ok, well then, let's look at the manner of murder for each," Maybel said. She drew a little building underneath Jennifer's stick figure. She drew a triangle pool under Alice's photo and a washing machine under the cord that hung over the whiteboard. Last, she drew a little plastic bag under Mandy's stick figure.

The ladies sat there staring at the board for a minute, but no clear answers jumped out at them. Maybel asked if anyone wanted decaf coffee, and both ladies said they'd love some. Celeste grabbed a chocolate thumb print cookie. Janet took two cookies topped with sprinkles, and Maybel ate a pizzicati cookie filled with raspberry jam. As they sipped their coffee in Maybel's dimly lit den, something occurred to Celeste. "You know, none of these victims were killed in their own places, nor were any of them shot, stabbed or poisoned. Those would be more common ways to kill someone."

"Good point, but how does that help us solve this?" Maybel asked.

"I don't know. It's just an observation. And what about the locations of all the murders…the roof, the pool, the laundry room and the trash shoot. I wonder if the locations have anything in common besides the lack of security cameras…like all these areas could be accessed easily by non-residents. Also, I'm still wondering if there is any common thread between Mark and the other victims. He's the only male victim. We know so little about him other than his regular laundry schedule…which if anyone else knew his schedule, would have made it easy for them to tamper with the cord to the dryer right before he used the laundry room that day."

"Bingo!" Maybel shouted. She puffed out her chest and remembered her power as HOA president. "That's why I used my master universe key to get into his place and look around."

Celeste asked, "Your what?"

"Years ago, as you know, I was the best board president of Regal Palms. As president, you are given a universal master key that can get into any unit in the building in case of emergencies like fires. That's why residents aren't allowed to install their own locks on their units and must use the HOA approved locks. It's in our by-laws from years ago."

Celeste frowned as she realized what Maybel was getting at and asked, "You broke into Mark's place?"

"That's not the point, dear. Don't worry about that. The point is I found some interesting things I think you both will want to be made aware of," Maybel said and looked like she'd put a feather in her cap.

Janet asked, "Does this mean Vick has a universe key too?"

"Yes, that moron has one as well," Maybel answered.

Celeste corrected them, "I think it is just called a master key, or a universal key, not a universe master key. It's not for the whole universe, just this building." She knew Maybel's HOA presidency was one of the most important things in the world to her and tended to get carried away. She asked, "And Maybel, why didn't you give your master key back when you were done with your two terms as president?"

"Dear, that's not important right now. Do you want to know what I found or not?" Maybel asked defiantly.

"Sure," Celeste said and took another sip of her coffee.

Maybel wrote the word "**SEX**" on a post-it and slapped it over the drawing of the building. She circled the building, pointed to it and said, "I found naughty photos. Ladies, the sex is going on all over this building!"

Celeste let out a sigh. She thought the night turned out to be more like Maybel's game of Regal Palms Pictionary rather than a murder board. "Oh boy," she said under her breath.

Janet leaned forward and said, "Tell us more."

Maybel looked victorious and said, "Mark really lived in the gutter. Somehow, he took naughty photos of Vick and Jennifer, Billy and Jennifer, and Jennifer and some other men I couldn't identify. And ladies, let me tell you, Jennifer was into some really kinky stuff!"

Celeste scolded, "Maybel, you shouldn't kink shame her either."

Maybel shook her head and said, "Dear, I'm sure I'm too old to be limber enough to kink shame somebody…whatever that is."

"Even if you had a key to Mark's place, how did you find the pictures? I'm sure the police searched his place," Celeste wondered.

"Years ago, I knew the former resident of Mark's unit. You know, I've been here since 1958. I know a lot about this building," Maybel said.

"We know," Celeste replied.

"Anyway, the former resident installed some built-in bookcases—kind of like what you have, dear. However, hers had a secret compartment that Vera, that's the lady that used to live there, hid her family jewels in. She was a good friend of mine and confided in me. She said if anything ever happened to her, I was to make sure her kids knew about the jewelry. Well, eventually she moved out, went to that retirement home Shady Sunset, and took her jewelry with her. But after Mark and Mandy died, I got to thinking and remembered the secret compartment. So…this morning I just simply used my master universe key and went into his place and looked in the secret compartment." Maybel whispered, "That's where I found the photos."

Janet wondered, "Isn't that tampering with evidence or interfering with a police investigation?"

"Or breaking and entering," Celeste added.

"It's not my fault if the police searched his place and didn't find them. I will tell the police about the compartment after our meeting tonight…and I left the photos where I found them. I wore gloves too," Maybel said.

"If there are compromising photos of Billy and Jennifer, I get why that would present a problem for Billy. But Vick is single, and I would think he'd probably be proud he 'intercoursed' with a young pretty woman like Jennifer," Celeste said making air quotes.

Maybel explained with a smile on her face, "The photos reveal that Vick is a very hairy man, dear. If those photos got out, it could be very embarrassing for Vick."

Celeste felt a bit annoyed, set down her coffee cup on a coaster and asked, "You're basing all of this on some hairy ass photos?"

"Dear, it's not his ass in the photos. And let me tell you, he's hairier than a gorilla on Rogaine," Maybel went on and whispered, "I mean, he has hair *everywhere* except for where he needs it." Maybel pointed to her head. "He's so hairy…poor Jennifer probably got rug burns from trying to…intercourse…at *it*." Maybel crinkled her nose up again and shook her head.

Celeste and Janet stared at Maybel. Celeste frowned.

"As I said ladies, all roads lead back to Vick." Maybel put the cap back on the pen and clicked it closed.

Celeste abruptly stood up and said, "We've really digressed, and I don't think we're going to get anywhere this evening. Let's just call it a night." She stepped out from behind the coffee table and started to leave the room. She turned to Janet and asked if she needed to walk Janet back to her place for safety reasons. Janet looked at her watch and let her know her husband would come get her soon and walk her back. "Ok, and Maybel thank you for the food, and promise me you will call Detective Bahn and let him know about the secret compartment in Mark's bookshelves. I know you have his number."

"Well, I know you have his number too, dear. What with all your secret conversations you have with him. I think—"

"That's not the point. Don't worry about that. Just promise me you will call him and tell him," Celeste said interrupting her.

"I promise," Maybel agreed. "Do you want to take your whiteboard back?"

"No, keep it for a while," Celeste said and walked back to her condo.

Chapter Eighteen

The List

Celeste changed into her pajamas and thought about the evening. She knew Maybel meant well, but the murder board proved to be unproductive. She felt bad for snapping at her, but the stress of what was going on in the building and the fatigue from pressure at her job was getting to her. She turned on her television and crawled into bed. Her cell phone plugged into the charger rang. Maybel.

"Hi dear, I have something else I have to tell you. I didn't want to say anything while Janet was here, but there was a photo of her husband Jack with Jennifer," Maybel said.

Celeste remembered Janet and her husband lived on the fifth floor. Maybe all the rumors were true, and maybe Janet knew. That might have been why she seemed so annoyed. "Oh no," Celeste said.

"Yeah, and I invited her to my murder board meeting because I wanted to see how she would react to everything. I mean Mark could have been trying to blackmail Jack, and then Janet found out and killed them both," Maybel said.

"That seems far-fetched. I mean, what about Alice and Mandy?"

"I never told you this, but Janet cheats at poker, and Alice caught her one time. They had a horrible fight," Maybel explained.

"And Mandy?"

"I don't have an answer for that. Perhaps we have more than one murderer in the building like you speculated," Maybel said.

"Maybel," Celeste let out a deep breath and said, "I think all this murder is going to our heads. I think we're seeing suspects where there aren't any. I think we both need to get a good night's sleep and talk about all of this later." Celeste and Maybel said goodnight for the evening.

Celeste put her phone back on the charger, turned out the light and went to sleep. Several hours later, she jolted awake. Her heart raced. She caught her breath and looked at the clock. It was 12:30 a.m. She thought about the parking spot waiting list.

She reached for her cell phone and sent Detective Bahn a text: **Are you awake?**

She held her cell phone and felt a little stupid. She heard her phone bing and looked at it: **Yes I am. Are you wearing that nightie?**

She laughed and texted back: **I think I might know why someone is killing people here and what the common thread is.**

She felt embarrassed again. This seemed so far-fetched, and he'd never believe her.

Her phone binged again: **Why?**

She took a deep breath, let it out and typed: **For a parking spot**

Bahn: **What?**

She explained further by texting: **Our building has a waiting list for reserved parking spots in our underground structure. A couple of months ago when I saw it, there were 18 people on the waiting list. But now there will only be 16 people on the waiting list because Mandy and Mark were both on the list. New residents sometimes have to wait a few years before they get a spot.**

Celeste sat in the dark and waited.

Bahn texted back: **Interesting. But what about Alice and Jennifer?**

Celeste fingers typed as fast as she could: **They weren't on the waiting list, but they were both living by themselves, and now their places are being sold. The new buyers will go to the bottom of the waiting list. They won't get Jennifer or Alice's spots. That's how it works. Essentially these four murders freed up four parking spaces**

Another very long pause and then Bahn texted back: **Ok we'll check out the waiting list and we'll see what we can come up with.**

Celeste breathed a sigh of relief. **Thank you**

Bahn texted back**: No problem. Now get some sleep kid :)**

Vick

Victor Arnold, also known as Vick Arnold, always wanted to be a cop. He failed the academy twice. He settled for being a security guard. He was twice divorced, and truth be told, he didn't really like women that much. They were all a bunch of nags you could never make happy. Over the years Vick developed a greasy comb-over and bit of a pot belly. He thought he was still quite a catch for the woman who wasn't shallow. Vick moved to Regal Palms about ten years ago after his second divorce. Vick's father owned the condo at Regal Palms as a rental property. He felt sorry for his son and allowed him to move in. Vick then took a job as a night watchman at the local mall in Sunshine Beach. He didn't mind working nights—less people to deal with.

He drove a midnight blue Crown Vic. He always said, "I'm Vick that drives a Crown Vic." No one else ever thought that was as clever as he did. Vick loved his Crown Vic and took meticulous care of it. He changed the oil once every three months, took it in for routine service every six months, and washed and waxed it every two weeks. The car was an extension of himself and housed his colt 45 in the glove compartment.

He got home from work on a crisp November Sunday morning around 5 a.m. while it was still dark out. He pulled into his designated parking spot in the cement underground lot and left the engine running. He loved the sound of that engine, and it usually purred like a kitten. That morning he heard a little bit of a rattling sound, probably caused by a loose belt. It would need to be tended to immediately. He put the Crown Vic in park and popped the hood. He grabbed the flashlight sitting on the passenger seat. There wasn't much light in the parking lot that time of morning. He walked to the front of his car and observed that everything looked clean and in order. He took a deep breath and smelled the engine. The scent of warm oil and gasoline was intoxicating to him.

Suddenly, his Crown Vic leapt forward. He stumbled back. God damn! He heard the flashlight hit the ground, and he felt his body press against the cold cement behind him. He heard his engine rev. The car continued to put pressure on him pining him against the wall. He tried to cry out but could barely make a sound. He let out a cough and could feel his stomach being crushed. The bile rose in his throat. He heard his spine crack.

The Crown Vic he'd taken such meticulous care of turned on him and almost drove him to his grave. Right before he passed out from the pain, he heard the clickety clack of high heels smacking the cement in the underground parking lot...

Chapter Nineteen

Velocity and Trajectory

Celeste looked forward to a relaxing Sunday. Maybe I'll do some shopping she thought as she got ready for her day. She headed to the kitchen to make a protein shake for herself, when someone knocked at the door. She knew it couldn't be good. She looked out the peek hole and saw the top of Maybel's head.

Maybel was panicked and out of breath. "Sweet Jesus! It isn't Vick!"

Celeste asked, "What isn't Vick?"

"The murderer isn't Vick. Someone tried to run Vick over with his own car in the parking lot early this morning!" Celeste noticed as Maybel spoke, she got teary eyed. "Now dear, you know I never much cared for Vick. I sometimes call him 'Vick the prick', and I may have started some rumors about him because he's the worst president we've ever had, but he doesn't deserve to die…especially if he isn't the murderer."

Celeste felt the room swirling around her. She'd tried to process what Maybel said. She felt woozy and sat down on the couch. Maybel rushed over and sat down next to her. They both sat there silently for a few minutes. Celeste realized she was holding her breath. She let it out and took another deep breath in. She also realized she was shaking. A shark lurked among them, she thought. Celeste could barely hear her own voice when she spoke, "Maybel this has got to end."

"I know, dear. This is insane. There is a serial killer loose in our building!"

"There are no security cameras in the garage either," Celeste said thinking out loud and rubbed her face. "Maybel, you might think this sounds crazy, but I think someone is killing for a parking spot."

Maybel frowned. "Who would do such a thing? They'd have to be a psychopath."

Celeste felt sick. "Tom Fitzpatrick is on the waiting list for a spot and so is Billy. Plus, I heard Tom sent a threatening email to Mandy Vu who was also on the waiting list."

"Ah, that's right. Janet lives on Tom's floor, and she heard him arguing with Mandy," Maybel said.

They sat there a while longer in silence until finally Maybel asked if Celeste needed breakfast. Celeste didn't go shopping that day. They went over to Maybel's house, and she made them omelets and coffee. After getting a little food in her stomach, and a second cup of coffee, Celeste began to think clearly. She thought she'd better let Brian know about Tom and Billy being on the parking spot waiting list.

She excused herself and reminded Maybel to keep her door locked. Celeste went back over to her place and sent a text to Detective Bahn that read: **I heard about Vick Arnold. By the way, Tom Fitzpatrick is on the parking spot waiting list and so is Billy Cheng.**

She didn't get a response back. I'm sure he's busy she thought.

Celeste felt emotionally exhausted and decided to lay down. She went in her bedroom, locked the door, and closed her curtains. She closed her eyes and must have dozed off but didn't remember when. She felt a little refreshed by her nap.

Checking her phone, she found a text from Detective Bahn that read: **Thanks for the tip. I had already checked the waiting list and saw that Fitzpatrick and Cheng are on it. We dusted Vick's car for fingerprints early this morning. Waiting for results now.**

Celeste felt a sense of relief that Detective Bahn was on the trail. She felt a little paralyzed by fear. Nowhere in the building was safe anymore. She picked up a book to read hoping it would give her mind a break. It didn't. She'd read the same paragraph three times and still had no idea what it said. She heard another knock at the door and practically jumped out of her skin. She got up, went to the door, looked out the peek hole, and saw the top of Maybel's head.

Maybel carried a plate with foil over it. "You know I bake to pass the time," she said and handed Celeste the plate.

Celeste could smell it and smiled. "Banana bread?"

"With chocolate chips," Maybel added.

Celeste couldn't resist. "Let's have some," she said and went over to the kitchen to make some coffee to go with it.

"I feel guilty that I dislike Vick so much," Maybel said and took a sip of her coffee.

Celeste spread some butter on her banana chocolate chip bread. "Vick doesn't always make himself very likeable, and that's not your fault," Celeste said trying to comfort Maybel in the madness.

"And to think—I thought Vick was the one killing everyone. I was so sure of it," Maybel said and shook her head.

"I think this is a time when we can't be too careful or trust anyone," Celeste said. "Could it have been an accident? Could Vick have gotten out of his car and forgot to put it in park?"

"No way it was an accident. Witnesses said he'd been smashed up between his car and the parking lot wall. Someone had to have had their foot on the accelerator in order to get that much velocity," Maybel said.

"Witnesses? You spoke with witnesses?" Celeste asked.

"Don't worry about them now, dear," Maybel said. Celeste didn't push any further. She knew from experience Maybel had an excellent gossip chain going. Celeste wondered if the murderer got scared off by someone else in the parking lot. People come and go all the time down there. Maybel and Celeste chatted for a while longer about all the people trying to move out of the building. "Well, I'm on a fixed income, but if I sold my place, I would cash in on a lot of equity," Maybel said. She got up and put her coffee cup and plate in the sink. "I'm going to get going. One of my shows is going to be on soon," Maybel said and left.

Celeste sat back down on the couch and tried reading again. This time she forced herself to concentrate. After about an hour of reading, she stopped. She heard her phone bing. She read the text from Detective Bahn: **We found Tom's fingerprints on the flashlight that was found by Vick's body. We're bringing him in.**

Celeste called Maybel and told her. She knew Maybel would be relieved. "Well, that's good news!" Maybel said. Their conversation was brief. Maybel's TV was very loud.

Celeste decided to go for a walk on the beach. Celeste put on her walking shoes, grabbed her keys and phone, and headed out. The fresh air felt great on her face and arms, and she could smell the salt air. She headed down Pacific Boulevard and walked until she hit the beach. She took off her shoes, rolled up her pantlegs, and walked out onto the sand. It felt cool under her feet and between her toes.

Celeste didn't go to the beach very often, but that day it felt right. She walked until the dusky sky trimmed the shoreline. She loved the sound of the ocean at night. The roar of the waves seemed louder in the dark somehow. The ebb and flow soothed her. She stood still for a bit and felt chilled by the breeze. It rustled her hair and kissed the back of her neck. She closed her eyes and could feel the sound of the waves tickle her ear drums. As Celeste stood at the edge of the water, it rolled in and touched her toes. She felt the dead haunt her. They didn't have justice. She knew on instinct the shark still lurked among them.

After the mysterious ocean night air cleared her head, she wondered a few things. If Vick was run over by his own car, what did his flashlight have to do with anything? Was he hit in the head with it? Did someone pretend they were going to help him with his car?

Celeste got colder by the minute and decided to head back. She got to the warm cement, brushed off as much sand as she could, and put her shoes back on. She made her way back up Pacific Boulevard, passing some of the local restaurants and shops as she did. She felt tempted to do some shopping but talked herself out of it. You don't need any more clothes, she thought. Her stomach growled at her, and she wanted to stop to get something to eat but remembered she didn't bring her wallet.

Traffic on the street rushed past her as she approached her building. She looked out into the road at the spot where Jennifer landed. Maybel pointed it out the day it happened. Celeste could still see the spot from the blood on the street. If you didn't know what it was, you'd think it was an oil stain. Now cars raced over it all day long, as if nothing happened. She stood there staring at that spot and shook her head. She looked all the way up to the top of the twelve-story building and thought about Jennifer jumping off the roof. She looked back down at the spot on the street, back up at the building, and then back down at the spot. The trajectory was wrong. If she jumped, she would have landed straight down on the sidewalk, not all the way out on to the street. Someone threw her off the roof.

Celeste felt someone staring at her and turned away from the street and towards the sidewalk in front of her building. There she saw Detective Bahn walking towards her from the direction of the pavilion. He carried two grocery bags, and a smile was plastered on his handsome face. "Fancy meeting you here," he said.

Chapter Twenty

Winner, Winner, Chicken Dinner

The overhead streetlights illuminated Detective Bahn's hair like a halo. Celeste was a bit startled when she saw him approaching her on the street. "Detective Bahn, what are you doing here? Tell me there hasn't been another murder."

"It's Brian, and no, thank God. I just wanted to chat with you." He held up the grocery bags. The only thing that could rival the strength of his libido was his appetite. "I parked at the pavilion again, and I couldn't get through there without buying something. Are you hungry?"

"You read my mind."

They walked side by side up the pathway to the building, and they made their way through the lobby and over to the elevators. She hit the up arrow and waited an awkward minute. Finally, the elevator dinged, and the doors opened. Detective Bahn extended his hand out to indicate for Celeste to go first. Doors closed and the elevator clunked into its slow ascent. She thought she smelled fried chicken.

"And potato salad and biscuits," he said when asked.

He followed her as they walked to her place. "Should we invite Maybel?" She wasn't sure why she asked that. She knew he wanted to be alone with her. Maybe that was why she asked…

"Next time," he said.

She dropped her keys on the bar counter and turned on the lights. "I'll get some plates."

Detective Bahn followed her into the kitchen and set the bags down on the counter. She pulled plates from her cabinet, got out forks and spoons, and he took all the food out of the bags. He'd also gotten some three-bean salad which was Celeste's favorite. Celeste wondered if Maybel told him that.

She handed him a plate so he could dish up first. She dished up her own plate and set it on the bar in front of one of the bar stools to indicate that's where they would sit. She thought if they sat at the table, it would feel like they were on a date.

It turned out Detective Bahn was a fast eater. She knew she should be trying to make conversation with him, but satisfying her hunger was first. The three-bean salad had a good tang to it from the vinegar dressing and that cut through the greasy fried chicken. They chewed in silence.

Bahn got up and got himself seconds.

"There is butter in the refrigerator if you want to put some on your biscuits," she said, and he poked around and took what he wanted. "You arrested Tom?"

"Yep," he said, pulled apart a chicken wing and devoured it. He dropped the picked clean bones down on his plate.

Celeste put her fork down. "I know you probably aren't supposed to tell me anything, but I was wondering if he admitted to any or all of the murders?"

Bahn stopped worrying a long time ago about what to tell Celeste and what not to tell her. He simply trusted her. "He did not. He denied it all, but like I texted, we have his fingerprints on the flashlight," Bahn said and shoveled a huge bite of potato salad into his mouth.

Celeste asked, "Was Vick hit on the head?"

Detective Bahn put his fork down and looked at Celeste. He thought about how pretty she was. He also knew that while he was comfortable with her, he still needed to be careful how much he told her. "At first inspection, we didn't see any blunt force trauma to his head," he said.

Celeste frowned. "Then what does the flashlight have to do with anything?"

"It puts Fitzpatrick at the scene of the crime," Bahn said and gnawed on a chicken thigh.

Celeste didn't want to argue, but she had to ask, "Does it really? Or does it just show that at some point in time, Tom used or held Vick's flashlight?"

"Well, that's a good point, but it's about all we have to go on right now. This has been an extreme situation here, and the police chief pushed us to make an arrest. There is still very little physical evidence."

Celeste asked, "Did Tom have an explanation for why his fingerprints were on Vick's flashlight?"

"He said he'd helped Vick change his alternator a few weeks ago," Bahn said.

"Well, that would be easy enough to check out if it's true…like if Vick had a receipt for an alternator. I just think the theory about killing for a parking spot is kind of far-fetched."

"But it's your theory," Bahn replied.

"I know," Celeste said and laughed.

Bahn got up and took his plate, her plate, and the silverware to the sink. He washed the dishes and put them in the drainer. She got up from the bar stool and moved over to the couch. He followed her over to the living room and sat down in her cushy leather chair.

She tucked her legs up under her and put her arm against the back of the couch. "I don't want to be a ghoul about this, but may I ask what Vick's body looked like at the scene of the crime?"

Detective Bahn paused for a moment staring at her. He felt Celeste was too delicate to hear the truth about some things, but he didn't want to lie. He took a deep breath. "The EMT said his stomach was smashed in. Not a pretty sight. They took him to the emergency room this morning. The doctor said it's bad, but they think there is a good chance he will survive."

Celeste asked, "So the flashlight really wasn't the weapon that injured him, correct?"

"Correct," he said.

"Was it found in the car?"

"On the ground by car," Bahn answered.

"There is something bothering me," she said.

He tilted his head to the side. "And what would that be?"

"Well, tonight when I was walking back from the beach, I was looking at the spot on the street where Jennifer landed," Celeste said.

"Uh huh…" He stared at her, waiting.

"If she jumped off the building, she probably would have landed straight down on the sidewalk, because she wouldn't have had enough momentum to fling her body out into the street. Someone would have had to have thrown her off the roof for her to land where she landed."

"Yes, we already established Jennifer was murdered. She was strangled before someone threw her off the roof. I thought I told you that," Bahn said.

"Yeah, you did, but if she was thrown off the roof, I don't think Tom could have done it," Celeste said.

Bahn rubbed his chin. "And why is that?"

"Maybel once told me that he's a vet and served in Afghanistan. He was injured and has nerve damage in his arm. He basically can't use his left arm. I don't think an essentially one-armed man could throw a body off the roof with that much force," Celeste said.

"Well, at least we can get him on Mandy's murder. The murders here at this building have left so little physical evidence," he said again.

"But even to strangle Mandy with only the use of one hand seems impossible. Do you really think Tom did it?"

"He's denying any involvement," Bahn said.

"But do you think he did it?" Celeste pushed.

Bahn knew Celeste was right, but he said, "I think it is likely he did. However, I will say that I have interrogated a lot of suspects in my day, and Fitzpatrick didn't crack, at all. He also lawyered up pretty quick."

"Something just doesn't feel right," Celeste said.

"I know. That's why I stopped by. I wanted to warn you again to keep your doors locked, don't let your guard down, and keep your eyes and ears open," Bahn warned.

Celeste nodded. "Maybel made some banana chocolate chip bread. Would you like some for dessert?"

His eyes lit up. "I love banana bread!"

Celeste chuckled and said, "So that's a yes." She stood up. "Do you want some coffee to go with it?"

"Caffeinate me please. I have a long night ahead of me."

Celeste went into the kitchen, made him a cup of coffee and sliced off a piece of banana bread for him. "Do you take cream or sugar in your coffee? Because I don't have either. I only have almond milk and honey."

"That's ok. I take it black," he said.

She brought his dessert and coffee over and handed it to him. Balancing the plate with the banana bread on his knee, he took the mug of coffee and sipped. "You're not having any?"

"I had three cups of coffee today already so, no. I can get aggressive if I have too much caffeine," Celeste said and giggled. "Do you think it is possible that not all the murders were committed by the same person?"

"So, we're back on that, are we," he said and smiled.

"We never left it."

"Yes, I think it is entirely possible that not all the murders were committed by the same person. Especially now that you told me about Fitzpatrick's arm. Maybe we should bring in Billy Cheng and question him about Jennifer again," he said. They both sat there in silence, and then Bahn drank some more of his coffee and took a bite of the banana bread. "Oh, this is good!"

"You should tell Maybel that. She loves talking to you. She thinks you look like Steve McQueen," Celeste said with a grin.

"The first time I met Maybel was when we were out on the street after Jennifer's murder. She ducked under the caution tape, walked right up to me, and asked if I needed help 'securing the perimeter'," Bahn said with a chuckle as he used air quotes with his free hand.

"She could do it too. Don't underestimate her," Celeste said.

"Speaking of Jennifer, there were rumors that she had just gotten engaged. We went through her phone records again thoroughly, and there was one number she'd texted and called that could have been the guy," Bahn said dangling this tidbit in front of Celeste.

Celeste sat up straight and asked, "And? Who was it? Or can you say?"

"We couldn't trace the number to anyone. It was a burner phone."

Celeste slumped back down disappointed.

"There were also some interesting texts on Mandy's phone too."

Celeste's eyes widened. "From the same untraceable number?"

Bahn shook his head. "No. It was a second untraceable number."

"Can't be just a coincidence," Celeste said.

"Yeah, I have officers searching Tom Fitzpatrick's condo and Vick Arnold's condo right now. When I'm done here, I need to go over there."

That statement made it clear their dinner wasn't a date. "Well, I don't want to keep you from important business," Celeste said and stood up. She held her hand out for the plate and Bahn handed it to her and got up. She walked over to the kitchen, with him quickly following her. She put the plate in the sink and turned and took his cup.

"Hey…you seem upset. What's wrong?"

Celeste didn't know. She didn't want to date a cop again so why should she care if their dinner was a date or not? All this murder made her feel on edge. She hated how unresolved it still felt. "Nothing. I think I'm just frazzled from all of this. We're all just sitting ducks here! I mean, four murders? One attempted murder? And no real physical evidence," she said and frowned at him.

"Not yet, but we are diligently searching. I assure you that. I'd love to tell you not to worry, but this is a bad situation still," he said and touched her arm. His brows knit together, and he looked as worried as she felt.

"Did Maybel tell you about the secret compartment in Mark's bookcase?" Celeste searched his face.

"She did, and we checked it out. I shouldn't tell you this, but it was full of dirty photos. It was like a photo album of Jennifer's lovers."

Celeste asked, "Do you have any idea how Mark ended up with them?"

"He lived on the third floor next to Jennifer's condo. He drilled a small hole in the wall and—"

Celeste interrupted. "Oh God! Ok, I got it."

"Yeah, he was a real voyeur," Bahn said.

Celeste asked, "How did Jennifer not know there was a hole in her wall?"

"Her side of the wall with the hole had wallpaper on it. It's a busy print so the hole wasn't obvious, and it's not very big."

Celeste asked, "What about on Mark's side of the wall? You guys didn't see the hole when you searched his place?"

"He put a painting of a naked chick over it, and we didn't think to look behind it on the first search. After Maybel told me about the secret compartment in his place, we went back over everything and found it," Detective Bahn explained.

Celeste nodded and let out a deep breath. "You should probably get going."

"Yeah, I have work to do, and it's past your bedtime," he said grinning and winked at her.

She ignored him and moved towards her front door. She walked through her kitchen and around to the hall with her bookcase on it. Birino chirped, and they both looked up at him. He was perched on the top shelf again. One of the lights from her track lighting shined right where her little birdie like to nestle himself for a nap.

"Hey little fella," Bahn said to him. Birino fluttered his wings and chirped again.

"When we open the front door, we need to be careful not to let him out. Sometimes he likes to try to escape," Celeste said.

The Cheshire cat smile made another appearance on Bahn's face. "Why would he ever want to escape you?"

Celeste wondered if he was flirting with her. "Good luck. I hope you find something helpful," she said sincerely.

"Me too. Goodnight Celeste, and remember to lock both your doors." He saluted her and walked off.

She closed the front door quickly, locked it, and checked it twice. And then checked it a third time. She turned out her lights, went to her bedroom, locked that door and checked it again.

Chapter Twenty-One

Search and Seizure

Bahn stood with his hands on his hips facing a young police office with a buzz cut and asked, "Nothing? You didn't find anything?" They were at Tom Fitzpatrick's condo on the fifth floor. Tom and Vick both had condos on the east side of the building with a mostly industrial view.

"No, we haven't found much of anything really. Tom's place is clean and orderly. Not much paperwork of any kind. Normal kitchen. Nothing in the trash. He does have a few guns, but they are all registered to him, and none of them look like they've been fired recently. We can take in his computer and have forensics check out the hard drive." The young police officer wanted to be as helpful as he could.

"Yeah, sure. What about Vick's place?"

The officer motioned to the place next door. "They are still over there right now."

"Thanks," Bahn said and headed over to Vick's. Two officers just finished up their search. Since Vick hadn't officially been ruled out as a suspect, Detective Bahn ordered a search of his place as well.

Vick's place, like Tom's, was a small one-bedroom condo, a nice bachelor pad. It didn't have the same view as Celeste's place and was smaller. He kept it clean and orderly.

"Nothing?" Bahn was ready to lose his cool.

"Yeah, we've gone through his trash, drawers, under his bed, his closet." The first officer at Vick's explained. He pulled his latex gloves off, clearly giving up.

The second officer said, "We did find a couple of magazine collections. He has a subscription to a cop magazine and a girlie magazine. There's a whole stack of them in the corner there." He pointed to the bedroom.

"Bring in the hard drive to his computer." Bahn barked and felt beyond frustrated.

The second cop asked, "Ok, do you want us to take any of the magazines?"

"No. Well, yeah maybe just a few…but put your gloves back on before you touch them." Bahn turned and walked out of Vick's condo. He knew what he needed to do next. He ascended floors five, six, seven, eight, nine, ten, eleven, twelve…ding. Boom, boom, boom, boom went the forceful and rhythmic knock on the brass door to the penthouse.

Lily opened the door clad in only a towel. She asked breathlessly, "Yes, can I help you?"

"Is your husband home?" Bahn was determined to get to the bottom of this.

"Yes, let me get him." She left the door opened and walked into the other room.

Detective Bahn stood in their foyer and looked around at the place. The view was stunning. The place was twice the size of Celeste's with a big open concept layout. They garishly decorated it in reds and black, but it still looked like money. A large picture of a dragon hung over their leather couch.

"Detective Bahn, what can I do for you again?" Billy Cheng asked as he walked out of the bedroom wearing only pajama pants. He was tall, lean and mean. He'd already been questioned by Bahn once and knew this couldn't be good.

"I need to ask you a few more questions," Bahn answered.

Lily walked out of the bedroom. This time she wore a blue romper. Bahn wasn't sure it was a good idea to question Billy in front of her and said so.

"I have nothing to hide from my wife Lily. You can ask me your questions in front of her." Billy Cheng was a man used to being in charge. As the Vice President of his father's company that dealt in imports and exports, he was cutthroat at the deal.

"Jennifer Riley—were you having an affair with her?" Bahn got right to the point.

"No," Billy replied.

"We have her phone records, and we know she was sending you nude photos and suggestive texts," Bahn said and kept the detail of Mark's photos of Billy and Jennifer to himself.

"That is true…and Lily is aware that happened," Billy said and remained cool.

"You deny any physical involvement with her?"

"Detective Bahn, I already answered that the first time you questioned me." Billy was still cool.

"I think you're lying. I think you had an affair with her. I think she threatened to tell your wife, you got angry at her, strangled her, and threw her off the roof." Bahn didn't break eye contact with Billy.

"I told you. I had nothing to do with her death," Billy said still cool.

"Then maybe your little wife here did it," Bahn pointed his thumb in her direction and hurled out the accusation like a tennis player lobs a ball over the net.

"No!" Lily screamed and lunged at Detective Bahn impulsively biting his thumb.

"Shit!" Bahn shouted and shoved her back.

This triggered a roundhouse kick out of Billy, but Bahn always light on his feet, moved back in time to only get clipped on the tip of his chin. In one swift motion, Bahn grabbed his gun, took the safety off, pointed it at Billy and commanded, "Stop! Hands up!" Bahn was the rare type of man whose heart rate went down when he drew his gun. If he'd practiced pulling his gun once, he'd practiced it a million times.

Billy froze. Lily screamed and cried and flailed about. "Lily! Stay!" Billy commanded and Lily froze.

Bahn got on his radio and asked for back up. Both Billy and Lily were taken in for assaulting a police officer. He began working on the warrant to search their place.

Chapter Twenty-Two

Grab the Bull by the Horns

After Celeste locked her doors as Bahn instructed her before he went to search Tom's place, she tossed and turned trying to fall asleep but was deep in thought. Tom Fitzpatrick was kind of an intense guy, but he hardly seemed like a killer. Yes, he had a temper, but that didn't make someone a murderer. While maybe he had something to do with Mandy's death, why on earth would he have drowned Alice? Or electrocuted Mark? And she already knew he couldn't have thrown Jennifer off the roof. Celeste began to think her parking spot theory wasn't too stupid after all, but who would kill for a parking spot? You'd have to be a total narcissistic psychopath.

Four souls in the building were taken, either by murder or accidents under very suspicious circumstances. Even though Detective Bahn arrested Tom, Celeste believed the murderer could still be on the loose. Did Billy Cheng murder Jennifer? Could Lily Cheng have murdered her? She thought there was a very good chance they weren't all committed by the same person. Celeste didn't pray very often, but that night she tried it. *God, please protect everyone living in this building. Please help Detective Bahn catch the killer. Please give peace to Jennifer, Alice, Mark, and Mandy's families. Please heal Vick of the injuries he endured, and please bring this to an end. Amen.*

Celeste's alarm went off the next morning while it was still dark out. Ugh…I hate Monday mornings, she thought. She sipped some strong coffee and got ready for work. She slipped into her wedge heels, and as she tied the belt attached to her pale blue dress, she could have sworn she heard the lock on her front door click. Her heart jumped. Birinio's cage squeaked. She walked out of her bedroom and into the hallway. Her next-door neighbor, Alex Graham, stood inside her condo staring at her with a toothy smile on his face…and gloves on his hands.

Alex whispered, "Hello Celeste."

"Alex, what are you-"

"What am I doing here? You gave me your key, remember Celeste? And I made a copy of it while you were out of town for Alice's funeral." He kept smiling and tilted his head to the side.

Oh God—it's him! Help me! Celeste felt her heart beating out of her chest and pounding in her ears. She couldn't move. Alex took a few more steps towards her slowly. She was frozen in fear.

"It's really quite sad what's going to happen to you, Celeste," he said sounding sympathetic as if he cared, but Celeste knew he didn't. He smiled again at her. He was the narcissistic psycho…the shark that lurked among them…and he was circling her.

"What's going to happen to me, Alex?" She was finally able to move and took a step back. She wasn't ready to meet her maker just yet.

He made a fake pouting face, tilted his head to the side again and said, "You're going to slip and fall in the shower. It's going to be a nasty fall too. You crack your head wide open."

Celeste knew she needed to keep him talking. "Did you kill Jennifer too?"

Alex laughed and said, "That dumb slut deserved to die. I did the world a favor. She was a *bitch*!"

God help me! "Were you engaged to her?" Celeste kept her voice calm but could barely breath.

"Why yes we were. How did you know? Your boyfriend the cop tell you?" Alex asked.

Celeste shook her head. "He's not my boyfriend."

"I thought if I asked Jennifer to marry me, she would let me use her parking spot. I had no intention of marrying her, but I thought the ring would persuade her to give me her spot. When

I asked, that stupid whore laughed at me." Alex's face changed as he spoke about her. It looked as if his glassy eyes rolled back in his head. "I strangled her and pulled that damn ring off her slutty finger. Then I tossed that piece of trash off the roof!" He breathed hard, and Celeste saw the gills of his murderous arousal flutter. He intended to take the breath of life from her.

For the first time Celeste noticed Alex's muscular biceps. She also knew there was no way she could outrun him, and her cell phone sat in the other room.

"I'm going to need for you to take your clothes off, Celeste," he said.

Celeste tried to brace herself for the attack. "Why?"

"You don't take a shower with your clothes on, do you?" he asked and laughed.

"Well, no, but I rarely take my clothes off in front of people, and I already took a shower." Celeste protested.

Alex took a knife from his pocket and said, "We can do this the easy way, or the hard way. You can commit suicide by slitting your dainty little wrists or fall in the shower and bang your head. I don't have a preference." He took another step towards her.

Oh God help me! "But Alice, what about Alice? She was a nice lady. Why would you drown her, Alex?"

"She had a parking spot for many years, Celeste. It was time for someone else to have a turn, and that old lady barely even drove anymore. The perfect opportunity presented itself when she was swimming alone. She didn't even see me coming when I swam up next to her," Alex said, and in Celeste's panicked state of mind she thought she saw a shark fin pop up on his back.

Celeste could feel her face burn and she thought about this sick bastard killing Alice for a parking spot. "And Mark?"

"Take your clothes off," he shouted.

Celeste began to tear up and said softly, "I just took a shower, Alex. I'd really rather not get back in." She could feel herself shaking.

"Celeste, you don't want to get blood all over your nice condo, do you? I know how neat and tidy you are. When you were out of town, I went through all your drawers and closets. I never did see your bird. I think I told you that. He's stuck up, just like you." Alex moved closer.

"Well, if I'm going to die, then you might as well tell me about Mandy." Celeste stalled, and she knew Alex knew she was stalling, but she also knew the guilty like to confess.

"Mandy was an idiot! Always droning on about the recycling and the dolphins. She was on the list ahead of me. Do you think I was going to let her park her MINI Cooper in my spot?" His sharp teeth were exposed by his laugh.

"No, I don't." Celeste shook her head. "Were you involved with Mandy too? Did you use burner phones for her and Jennifer?"

"Yeah, I like to keep the ladies separate. I didn't want to accidentally send a text to the wrong one, you know? Jennifer's phone was black, and Mandy's was red. It was going ok with Mandy and I too, until the night of the Halloween party. After dancing with me, she chased after that avocado cop all night and made a fool out of me." He shouted again, "Now take your clothes off!"

Celeste burned with anger when she thought about what Alex did to Mandy. She stalled and asked, "What about Vick?"

"Vick is an asshole—running around this place like he owns it and telling everyone what to do…him and his stupid wanna be cop car. You should have seen the look on his dumb face when I pinned him against the cement wall! I would have killed him too if it hadn't of been for that penthouse chick showing up in the parking lot during the attack." Alex circled closer towards Celeste. He shouted louder, "Now take your clothes off!" His eyes rolled back in his head for the attack, and his blood turned cold.

Suddenly, Celeste's front door opened. Alex turned to look. In an instant, with adrenaline running through her, Celeste grabbed the bronze bull bookend from the bookcase next to her, and as hard as she could, she hit him in the back of the head with it. She harpooned the shark. The angle was perfect since he was shorter than her. He hit the ground face down and went out like a light. "Maybel! Thank God!" Celeste breathed.

"Oh dear, are you ok?" Maybel held George's gun in her hand.

"Alex is the killer!" Celeste's breaths were rapid. "He just admitted to everything. What are you doing here by the way? Why did you come in?"

"Don't worry about that, dear. Right now, we need to restrain this sick bastard until the police get here. Do you have any rope?"

"I think I have some twine in my kitchen drawer," Celeste said and ran to get it.

Celeste called 911, and then with trembling hands, she texted Detective Bahn: **Alex Graham just tried to kill me he confessed to everything he's tied up at my place called 911 police otw**

Chapter Twenty-Three

The Wrap Up

Detective Bahn stood at the outskirts of Maybel's kitchen and sniffed the air. "It smells delicious, Maybel."

"Sausage and peppers…it's my mother's recipe," Maybel informed him.

"It's one of my favorites," Celeste said in reference to the dish Maybel pulled out of the oven—a mixture of Italian sausages, peppers, onions, potatoes and seasoning. The loaf of bread and bowl of salad already sat on Maybel's yellow Formica kitchen table. She invited Detective Brian Bahn over for Thursday night dinner to celebrate the killer being caught.

Maybel set the table with two place settings close together for Celeste and Brian on the opposite side she had put her own place setting. "Does anyone want wine?" She held up a bottle of Chianti. Everyone did. Maybel held her glass up. "A toast! Here's to that sick son of a B being locked up where he can't hurt anyone else."

"I'll drink to that," Celeste clinked her glass to Maybel's and Brian's.

Maybel brought the pan of sausage and peppers over to the table and set it down on a hot pad. "Well, dinner is ready. Let's eat," she said and waved her hand over the table.

"Maybel, this is absolutely delicious. I don't get a home cooked meal very often," Bahn said.

"I'm glad you like it. Celeste likes to cook too," Maybel hinted.

Celeste asked, "Brian, can you tell us anything about how the case against Alex is going?"

"Yes, and it's going very well." He stuffed a piece of buttered bread in his mouth, chewed twice and swallowed.

He barely even chews his food, Celeste thought to herself.

Bahn continued, "After the arrest and search of his place, we found a lot of physical evidence." He stabbed at his salad and speared a lettuce leaf. Rabbit food, he thought as he tasted the Italian dressing on the arugula.

"Ooooo! Like what?" Maybel sprinkled parmesan cheese on her salad.

"We found the two burner phones. Remember I was telling you Jennifer had been texting with someone we thought might have been her fiancé, but we couldn't trace it," he asked Celeste. Maybel gave her a look, now realizing they had more conversations she was not aware of.

Celeste ignored the look. "Yes, I remember. You also said Mandy texted with someone you thought she was involved with, so you found that burner phone too?" Celeste asked.

"Yes, and we found a diamond ring with Jennifer's DNA on it. We hit the jack pot," Bahn said.

"Sounds rock solid," Maybel joked.

Bahn went on, "Yeah, and it gets better. We found a bag at his place, just like the one found on Mandy's head Alex used to suffocate her. Both bags were from the art festival stamped with that organization's logo. Plus, we found wire strippers that we were able to pull some fibers off. Those fibers matched the wires from the dryer in your laundry room."

"Oh, that's fantastic," Celeste said and felt relieved. Even though they arrested Alex, she was having nightmares about him breaking into her condo. Those dreams coupled with her reoccurring stress dream of being eaten by a shark took a toll on her. She also feared they'd release Alex, and he'd come back. She didn't confide in anyone about it, but the whole mess was tormenting her.

"We were also able to trace a hair we found in Vick's car back to Alex," Bahn continued, "The only murder we didn't have any real physical evidence for was Alice's, but we'll have Celeste's testimony about Alex's confession."

"I'm going to bury that guy in court." Celeste took another big sip of her wine. She felt it relax her muscles. As she finished up her salad, she wondered why she didn't drink more often. She took a bite of Italian sausage and could taste the fennel in it.

"Sweet Alice, God rest her soul," Maybel said shaking her head. "I sure miss her, and so does Janet."

"The D.A. says it's a pretty solid case. Graham should go away for a long time," Bahn said.

"Thank the good Lord for that!" Maybel held her wine glass up again and toasted no one in particular. "We were all pretty freaked out. I still can't believe something like this happened here. This has always been such a great home to me. What is wrong with that kid, to think it was ok to murder four innocent people, for a parking spot?"

"He must have had a complete psychotic break. I wish we could have caught him sooner. That night we searched Tom Fitzpatrick's condo and didn't find anything, I went back to the station and took another look at the parking spot waiting list. I wanted to see who else besides Fitzpatrick was high up on the waiting list. Graham wasn't on the list, but a man named Martin Wright was on it. We were in the middle of contacting him when I got the text from Celeste. We found out later Martin owns the condo Alex Graham was renting."

Maybel was dismayed by the information. "He didn't even own his place, and he was killing for a spot? I don't even think I have words for that!"

"But if Martin got the spot, it would then go to his renter. I'm just glad it is over," Celeste said.

Detective Bahn spoke again, "I think Graham's lawyer is going to go for an insanity plea. The D.A. said they questioned some of

Graham's family members, and he has a history of mental illness. His Mother said he always had an inappropriate sense of entitlement to things that weren't his."

Maybel snorted in disgust. "Ugh! This was way beyond that!"

"I know. She also said when he was in middle school, he set fire to the shed in their backyard because she wouldn't let him store his bike in it," Bahn went on, "His father was abusive. Graham was a bed wetter until he was ten, and his father beat him every time it happened."

"The sins of the father…" Maybel's voice trailed off.

"And Graham's mother said one time when Graham was about fourteen and the family dog had an accident on the carpet, Graham beat the dog the death. That's when she knew something was really wrong with him," Bahn further explained.

"Geez…that's so sick," Celeste felt woozy thinking about it. "By the way, Maybel, I'd been meaning to ask you again, that morning Alex broke into my condo, what made you come over?" Celeste normally didn't push when Maybel told her not to worry about something, but her curiosity prevailed.

Maybel sat back in her chair and looked at both of them. "I don't know if I should say this in front of Detective Bahn, but since you asked, I will. That morning I was up early reading my bible like I normally do, and I heard a man's voice in your condo. You know the walls here are paper thin, and since I'm right next to you, I kept hearing him say 'take off your clothes', 'take your clothes off', and I got worried someone was trying to take advantage of you."

"And you decided to come over and make sure I was ok." Celeste smiled at her. Maybel really was a treasure and an answer to prayer.

"Well, yes dear. I figured if you wanted to take your clothes off, he wouldn't have to tell you so many times," Maybel said.

Celeste shuddered. "I still remember the look on his face. It gives me chills."

Detective Bahn put his hand on hers. "It will go away eventually," he reassured her.

Maybel smiled at Celeste. It was obvious to her that Detective Bahn cared for her.

"By the way, the cops who were the first responders to the 911 call said when they got to Celeste's place, Graham was hog tied. Which one of you ladies did that?" Bahn looked back and forth at both of them.

Celeste chuckled and replied, "That was all Maybel. I mean, it was my kitchen twine, but Maybel tied him up."

"I brought George's gun with me, but Celeste hit that psycho over the head before I could use it. Then I trussed him up like a Thanksgiving turkey! After what he did to Alice, he's lucky I didn't shove my turkey baster up his—"

"Ok! We got the idea," Celeste interrupted and laughed.

"Who wants dessert?" Maybel asked and got up from the table.

"I do," Detective Bahn said.

"You don't even know what it is yet," Celeste said.

"I know it will be great," Detective Bahn said.

"It's pistachio pie," Maybel said. "It was one of my husband's favorites. It has a pistachio nut crust, pistachio pudding filling, and whipped cream on top."

Bahn smacked his lips. "Oh man, I love pistachios. That sounds awesome."

"It is," Celeste confirmed.

Celeste made coffee for everyone, helped Maybel clear the table, and set out dessert. Sitting back at the table she asked about Vick. Maybel replied, "He's back at home and the doctors said he will make a full recovery. I might have to be nicer to him."

"Why start now?" Celeste joked. They sat and chatted over dessert and coffee for another hour before Celeste said she needed to get going. She needed to get up early the next day for work.

"I should head out too," Detective Bahn said and stood up with her. Celeste gave Maybel a big hug and thanked her for everything.

Detective Bahn walked Celeste to her door. She contemplated inviting him in, but she knew what he'd think the invitation meant. She decided against asking him in. "Thanks for coming to dinner. I think that meant a lot to Maybel."

"And you?"

Celeste asked, "And me what?"

"Did it mean anything to you?" Bahn stared into her eyes.

Her heart did a little leapfrog. "Of course," she said and looked down, feeling a little shy.

He ran his thumb across her jaw line and kissed her forehead. "Maybe one of these nights we can go out on a real date," he suggested throwing out the first spark.

"Maybe we could," she said. She felt the spark land on her and start to smolder there in the hallway on the ninth floor of the Regal Palms building built in 1958. The heat made Celeste Ravenna let her guard down just a little, and she felt a layer of ice melt off her.

The Cheshire cat grin pranced across his face again. He saluted her and turned to walk away. After a few steps down the hall, he turned back around and said, "You're in for a good time Miss Ravenna."

Celeste blushed, laughed and said goodnight. As she locked the door, she heard her phone bing. A text from Maybel read: **I'm glad he asked you out. You deserve love, dear.**

Celeste texted back: **How do you know he asked me out?**

Maybel replied: **Don't worry about that now, dear. Just have a good night.**

Celeste's Prelude

Celeste Ravenna loved the Regal Palms condo complex. The old building possessed an abundance of charm. When she first saw it, it stole a piece of her heart. As an independent woman, she worked very hard for many years to save up enough money to buy her own place. The day she moved in was one of the happiest days of her life. After she got the keys from her real estate agent, she sat on the floor of her empty condo, drank from a bottle of champagne, and cried tears of joy.

Now, she stood on the rooftop observation deck of the building erected in 1958 and looked out at the city…a city she loved. As the sun began to set, the wind from the cold dry November air whipped around her, and she wondered how something so horrible could happen at Regal Palms. A serial killer murdered four people in the building and attempted to murder Vick and her. Initially she was shocked by it, and then she was in denial about it. Now, while she stood there on the roof looking out at the ocean, the full realization of the evil deeds done sunk into her soul, and she shuttered from the inside out.

"Celeste?" She heard the hypnotically deep voice behind her. Earlier she texted Detective Brian Bahn and asked him to meet her on the roof. Celeste turned around and saw such a handsome man standing there. He tried so hard to help all of them. He looked worried. "Celeste, I got your text. Is everything alright?" She tried to speak but got choked up. He moved closer to her. "Tell me what's going on," his voice was full of concern.

"Brian, I can't...," her eyes filled with tears and so did his, "I can't live here anymore." She began to sob. He moved closer to her and embraced her. She continued crying. "He was living right next to me...he could have killed me," her voice shook.

Brian said gently, "I know." Celeste emotionally broke down on the roof of the Regal Palms building. Brian and Celeste both knew the post-traumatic stress kicked in and wasn't going away any time soon. Whether this self-reliant woman wanted to admit it or not, she was shaken to her core and needed this sturdy man to lean on. Brian continued to hold Celeste as she cried. "We'll get you through this, kid," he promised, and in the most simple-hearted way, he felt the call to protect her. But his effort to comfort Celeste had no effect on her, because the sharks in her mind already started to circle...

If you'd like to find out what happens next for Celeste, Brian, Maybel, and even Vick, look for a book coming soon called:

A Harbor of Resentment

About the Author

Drew Dunmoore is a California native and enjoys visiting local amusement parks. Drew has worked in the financial services industry for twenty years but has been obsessed with murder mysteries for more than thirty. This is Drew's first book. To find out more about what's next in this series, check out Drew's website at:

www.dunmooredisports.com

Readers can reach Drew at ddunmoore@gmail.com

Follow Drew on Instagram: @drewdunmoore

www.ingramcontent.com/pod-product-compliance
Lightning Source LLC
Chambersburg PA
CBHW070342010826
48976CB00017B/1141